A Horse Named Peggy

and other enchanting

character-building stories

for smart teenage boys who
want to grow up to be good men

by
Richard Showstack
Illustrated by
Eric Whitfield

BeachHouse Books
Chesterfield Missouri, USA

Copyright

Graphics Credits:
Cover by Dr. Bud Banis. Based on drawings by Eric Whitfield with text and enhancements by Dr. Bud Banis.
Publication date 2004
ISBN 1-1-888725-66-4 Regular print BeachHouse Books Edition
ISBN 1-1-888725-67-2 large print (20pt) MacroPrintBooks Edition

Library of Congress Cataloging-in-Publication Data
Showstack, Richard, 1950-
  A horse named Peggy and other enchanting character-building stories for smart teenage boys who want to grow up to be good men / by Richard Showstack.
    p. cm.
  Summary: A collection of four short stories about teenage boys who overcome the lack of self-confidence that accompanies a physical disability, take responsibility for their actions, and improve their lives.
  ISBN 1-888725-67-2 (large type MacroPrintBooks imprint : alk. paper) -- ISBN 1-888725-66-4 (regular print BeachHouse Books imprint : alk. paper)
  1. Children's stories, American. [1. Conduct of life--Fiction. 2. Self-realization--Fiction.] I. Title: Horse named Peggy. II. Title.
  PZ7.S559143Ho 2004
  [Fic]--dc22   2004017312

BeachHouse Books
PO Box 7151
Chesterfield, MO 63006
(636) 394-4950

www.beachhousebooks.c

Acknowledgments

Thanks to Donie Nelson, Patt Healy and J. T. O'Hara for their continuing support and encouragement.

Thanks to Dr. Laura Schlessinger for her inspiration.

Thanks to Dennis Prager and Larry Elder for making me think.

Thanks to Dr. Bud Banis for believing in me (and my writing).

And a special thanks to my wonderful and talented illustrator, Eric Whitfield, who (almost) never got mad as I asked him time and again to do new versions of his illustrations until they matched my vision of them.

Contents

A physical disability can be a challenge, but overcoming the lack of self-confidence that comes with it can be an even greater challenge...

A Horse Named Peggy

Alex watched enviously as the two kids zoomed down the street on their brand-new hundred-dollar metal scooters. The happy expression on their faces contrasted with the worried look on Alex's.

He was standing next to the new SUV parked in the driveway in front of his middle-class ranch-style home. Next to him on the ground was a canvas bag filled to the brim with CDs, tapes and electronic toys.

Alex was waiting for his mother to come out. He was worried because, after taking care of an appointment of her own, his mother was going to take him to the doctor again.

Alex's mother, Emily, came out of the house. A white single mother in her thirties, she was wearing her "dressed for success" business clothes.

"You got everything?" Emily asked him. "Your disks? Your Gameboy?"

"Yes, Mom," Alex replied grimly.

Emily helped Alex get strapped into the SUV.

"You have your tapes? They have a VCR."

Alex pulled the tapes out of his bag to show them to Emily.

"They're right here."

Emily got into the driver's seat of the SUV.

"I should be back in plenty of time to get you to your doctor's appointment."

She started the car, pulled it out into the street and started driving.

"Mom..."

Emily answered without taking her eyes off the road.

"Yes, dear."

"I don't wanna go to the doctor any more," Alex said forlornly.

Emily glanced at him in the rearview mirror.

"I know, dear, but just a few more tests and they'll know for sure."

Emily tore through the traffic while talking on her cell phone.

"Look, I just need to speak to your boss, that's all," she said into the phone. "Don't put me on hold!"

Just then another driver cut in front of her.

"Watch out, you idiot!" she yelled.

Then she said, "Damn!" and, annoyed, hung up the cell phone.

"Now I know Grandma and Grandpa don't have a computer, but if you get bored, you can always do your homework, OK?"

Alex made an "oh brother!" look with his face.

When they reached the front entrance of the "Shady Acres Retirement Community," Emily pulled up to the guardhouse and spoke to the guard through the open window of her car.

"I'm just gonna drop my kid off at my grandparents' house."

The guard waved her through.

The SUV with Emily and Alex in it screeched to a halt in front of Emily's grandparents' house.

Emily's grandparents (Alex's great-grandparents) were both in their eighties. They lived in one of the one-story units in the retirement community.

They were waiting in the living room of their house, which was decorated in a traditional (that is, old-fashioned) way. On the wall next to the fireplace were pictures of their children, grandchildren, and great-grandchildren. There were also many pictures and other objects on the mantle over the fireplace.

Grandpa was relaxing in "his" lounge chair with his feet up, reading a book. Grandma was seated nearby, doing some needlework.

Grandpa closed the book. "I just don't see what all the fuss is about these Harry Potter books!" he sighed.

The doorbell rang and then Emily opened the door and poked her head in.

"Hello? Anybody home?"

Grandma got up to greet them.

"Hi, dear! C'mon in."

In walked Emily and Alex, the latter dragging his canvas bag.

Grandma walked over to them.

"Hi, Grandma," Emily said as she hugged her grandmother.

"Hi, dear."

Grandma leaned down to hug Alex.

"And how are you, dear?"

"Hi, Grey-Granma," Alex responded solemnly.

"Come on in. Grandpa's in the living room."

Alex dropped his bag and went into the living room to greet Grandpa, who by now was seated upright in his chair.

Alex hugged him.

"Grey-Grandpa."

"Hello, kiddo — how are ya?"

Emily entered the living room and went over and leaned down and gave her grandfather a hug.

"Thanks so much. I hate to bother you…"

"Don't worry!" Grandpa replied. "It's our pleasure."

Emily walked over and gave her grandmother another hug, and then looked at her watch.

"Now I shouldn't be long… I'll be back as soon as I find out what kind of web site this guy wants me to design."

Then she went over and gave Alex a hug.

"You know my pager number, right?"

Alex made an of-course-I-do face and said, "555-5252."

Emily walked towards the door but then turned halfway back towards the two in the living room and waved.

"Bye, now!"

"Bye!" Alex and Grandpa responded.

Grandma closed the door behind her.

"I'll go start on lunch," Grandma said before exiting to the kitchen.

Grandpa was still seated in his chair with Alex standing at his knees. Alex didn't look happy all.

"Why the long face, pumpkin?"

"I have another 'pointment at the doctor's. I don't wanna go there any more — I'm scared."

"Gee, that's too bad...," Grandpa said.

Just then, a picture frame that had been on the mantle over the fireplace "flew" to the floor, surprising Alex...

"Oh!"

...and getting Grandpa's attention.

"That's OK," said Grandpa. "I'll take care of that later."

Grandpa thought for a moment and then gestured to his lap.

"Why don't you get comfortable, and I'll tell you a little story."

Alex settled into his lap.

"It takes place back during what was called the Great Depression."

"Why did they call it that, Grey-Grandpa?"

"Because the whole country was poor, but the farmers in the Midwest were especially poor..."

~ ~

In front of the room of the one-room schoolhouse stood Miss Wiggins, a conservatively attired "school marm" of about forty-five years old.

There were about a dozen children between the ages of six and thirteen in the schoolhouse. One of them, Billy Diangelo, was drawing a picture of a boy riding a horse. He was twelve-years-old, skinny but handsome.

"Billy Diangelo, are you listening to me?" Miss Wiggins called out.

Billy, startled, looked up at Miss Wiggins.

"Yes, ma'am," he replied. "You was jus' sayin' that we gotta study hard."

All of the other kids, except Carol Blair, laughed. Carol, also twelve-years-old, was seated near Billy. New to the community, she was cute but shy.

"Now, Billy, you know that's not what I was saying," Miss Wiggins scolded him. "I was just saying that I hope you all have a nice summer."

The kids were squirming uncontrollably.

"Settle down! It's not time yet," yelled out Miss Wiggins, but no matter how hard she tried, there was no calming her students. It was the last day of school before summer vacation, and they were as excited as a bunch of wild horses about to be released from a corral.

But for the children in the small farming community of Olympia, Illinois, the summer vacation did not mean months of free time. Times were bad and there was no extra money to take vacations or send the kids to camp.

Rather, the younger kids were expected to help out around the house, and the older children were expected to help bring in the crops.

Because of the Depression, many of the families in the county had already lost their land. Some had stayed to work as tenant farmers on the very land they used to own, but others had packed all their worldly possessions in whatever vehicle they could afford and had headed out west, hoping to find fresh soil in which to sink their roots.

Finally, the big hand reached the top of the clock, and it was time to go. All the students (except Billy and Carol) noisily fought to get out the door of the one-room schoolhouse, as if no one wanted to be the last one to leave.

Billy had walked with a limp ever since he had been thrown by a horse four years earlier, and he knew that if he tried to leave with the other students he would just get trampled.

Carol remained seated and watched Billy as he slowly stood up and gathered his things. He stuffed some papers into his pocket.

"You take care, now, Billy," Miss Wiggins called out to him.

"I will, Ma'am," allowed Billy without looking up as he gathered his belongings.

Miss Wiggins knew that, with his stiff leg, Billy couldn't help out on the farm like the other kids did, but she asked anyway:

"You got some work lined up this summer?"

"No, Ma'am," he uttered sadly.

As Billy started to move toward the door, he walked with an obvious limp — he couldn't fully extend his right leg because he couldn't straighten his right knee.

Miss Wiggins took a step towards him.

"If you want, I can ask Axton Twilly over at the store if he needs some help."

Billy continued towards the door without looking back at her.

"No thank you, Ma'am," Billy said sadly. "I'll jus' see what my ma wants me to do around the house."

Carol and Miss Wiggins exchanged looks.

"OK, Billy," said Miss Wiggins. "See you in the fall."

Billy exited without responding.

Miss Wiggins shook her head and then started to gather her things.

Carol walked up to the front of the class to talk to her.

"Thanks so much for everything, Miss Wiggins," Carol said.

Miss Wiggins gave Carol a hug.

"Oh, you're so welcome, Carol. You've only been here a month, but you're already my best student. You got any plans for the summer?"

"Nothing special. My aunt and uncle never had kids, so they don't know what to do with me."

"Well, I'm sure you'll think of something."

She looked towards the door of the schoolhouse.

"I just worry about Billy," Miss Wiggins said. "You think you might look out for him?"

Carol's face brightened up when she heard this.

"Oh, yes, Miss Wiggins! I'll watch out for him!"

In front of the schoolhouse, Billy picked up his hand-made wooden scooter from the ground.

Timmy and Earl, a couple of the boys who had just exited the school house, were playing catch with a ball.

"Hey, Billy," said Timmy in a sincerely friendly way. "Wanna play catch?"

Billy didn't say anything — he just gave Timmy a dirty look.

Timmy shrugged his shoulders and turned back to Earl, who shook his head.

"Watch this!" yelled Timmy as he threw the ball a long way.

As Billy watched the two boys run off after the ball, he was filled half with anger and half with envy.

Billy was about to step on his scooter when Carol came out of the front door of the schoolhouse and called out, "Billy!"

Billy answered without turning around to look at her.

"What?"

"I, uh, I just wanted you to know that, well... maybe we'll see each other at church some time.

"I s'pose," said Billy, still not looking at her.

And with that, Billy started off down the country road that ran in front of the schoolhouse, standing on the scooter with his stiff crooked right leg as he pushed along the ground with his good left leg.

Carol sadly watched him go off. Then she slowly descended the front steps of the schoolhouse and started to walk off in the same direction in which Billy had just headed.

Billy was happily sailing down the road on his scooter like a sea captain sailing across the open sea.

The one good thing about his disability was that it gave him an excuse for not working, and Billy loved the summer. Not only did it mean he could escape from school and the taunts of the other kids, but it also gave him more free time to daydream. On a summer day, he'd often find himself sitting alone by the stream, thinking not only about what might be but also about what might have been...

Billy had always loved his parents, and he had hoped to take over their farm when he grew up. But he had had to give up that dream when his father was killed in a tractor accident two years earlier.

Before, his family had been considered better off than most, but ever since his mother, Diane (nicknamed "Didi"), became a widow, they had barely been able to scrape by. They still managed to keep a few dairy cows, and a hired hand, Hector, but there was many a night when Billy, his mother and his grandmother Bess were grateful to have anything to eat at all.

To earn extra money, his mother did some sewing for the neighbors and occasionally did some maid's work for John Bartlett, the banker who held the mortgage on the Diangelo farm. (He was a widower himself, so he didn't have anyone at home to do the cleaning for him.) She didn't seem to mind — she claimed she was happy to get any work at all — but Billy had inherited his father's pride and it galled him to no end to think of his mother scrubbing some other man's floors.

But all those worries seemed far away now as Billy happily sailed down the country road on his scooter. Today, anything seemed possible.

But then Billy looked up and suddenly stopped.

On the top of a small hill overlooking the low area where Billy was, three boys were seated on horses and looking down menacingly.

Billy instantly recognized them, for he had had run-ins with them before. It was Arthur Bartlett and his two friends, Morton "Molly" Anderson and Walter "Wally" McCoy. They seemed to be lying in wait for him.

Arthur was two years older than Billy. He not only came from the richest family in the county, but he was also the best rider, and he knew it. He looked tall, proud and handsome sitting high atop his beautiful steed, and his companions Wally and Molly looked scruffy in comparison.

At first, Billy hadn't been able to understand why Arthur kept company with such scruffy characters as Molly and Wally, but after he got to know Arthur a little better, he understood that Arthur needed to hang out with boys meaner than himself so that he could shine by comparison.

Billy made a decision. He turned around and started pushing his scooter back down the country road in the direction he just came from.

The three boys on horseback kicked their horses and raced down the side of the hill towards Billy, who was pushing furiously on his scooter.

When the three boys on horseback suddenly appeared behind him, Billy kept pushing on his scooter, but at a slower speed than before.

Molly called out loud enough for Billy to hear:

"Well, lookee, here, Wally. If it tain't that little lame Diangelo boy!"

Wally added: "Why, I do believe you're right, Molly. I wonder where a little cripple like him could be goin' in such a hurry."

Billy showed by the expression on his face that their remarks had hurt him, and he lost his concentration and felt off his scooter.

Molly: "Well, will ya look at that! He cain't even ride a scooter! No wonder he cain't ride a horse!"

Billy got back on his scooter and, determined not to respond to any of their remarks, tried to continue down the road.

But then Arthur called out to him:

"What's yer hurry, Billy? Your mamma ain't home, y'know. She's over at my house, scrubbin' the floors!"

"I bet that's not all she's scrubbin'!" Wally cackled.

This stopped Billy in his tracks, and he turned around to face the three of them.

"You take that back, Wally McCoy," Billy said angrily.

"Or what?" snarled Wally.

"Or... Or I'll tell everyone what a no-account scoundrel you are!"

Arthur descended from his mount.

"Did you just insult my friend?" Arthur asked menacingly.

Arthur rolled up his sleeves as he walked towards Billy.

"Apparently your momma never taught you how to talk to gentlemen. I guess I'll just have to teach you some manners."

And with that, Arthur started to attack Billy.

From down the road, Carol watched in horror as the two boys fought.

But Billy, although smaller and weaker than Arthur (and lame in one leg) managed to get some good licks in return. In fact, Arthur was taking so much punishment that Molly and Wally got down from their horses to help him subdue Billy. They grabbed him and held him down on the ground.

Billy by now had a black eye, and his clothes were torn and bloodied.

"What shall we do with 'im, Arthur?" Molly asked.

Arthur, breathing heavily, wiped his bloody nose with the sleeve of his torn shirt.

"Nothin'," he responded.

He picked up Billy's scooter and broke it in two pieces over his knee. Then, with all his might, he threw one piece of the scooter far into the field on his left and threw the other piece far into the field on his right.

"There," said Arthur. "That should take care of him. Let 'im go. He's not worth the trouble."

Molly and Wally let go of Billy and then, along with Arthur, they remounted their horses.

The three boys gave Billy one more dirty look before riding off.

Billy pushed himself up with one arm.

Carol appeared and rushed over to help him.

"Oh, my gosh, Billy. Are you all right?"

But Billy shrugged off her offer of help.

"I'm all right. I don't need your help," Billy said as he stood up. "Or anyone else's help, neither!

"I was just trying to be friendly," said Carol, hurt.

"Maybe you're just trying to be friends with me 'cuz you don't have any friends," Billy said, brushing himself off.

This hurt Carol even more.

As she watched, Bill slowly made his way into one field and retrieved one piece of his broken scooter. Then Carol went into the other field and retrieved the other piece. She walked up to him, holding it in her hand.

"If you want, I can carry them for you," she offered.

But Billy angrily grabbed the piece out of her hand.

"I told you," he growled. "I don't need nobody's help!"

Billy then turned and started to walk slowly down the road, leaving Carol standing there.

"Just because you're lame, Billy Diangelo, doesn't mean you're better'n other people," Carol, now not only hurt but angry as well, called out. "Lots a people got problems, you know."

Billy was listening to what she was saying but he continued to hobble down the road with his back to her.

Carol continued: "You don't have to accept my help, but you can't keep me from walking with you. It's a public road, after all."

So the two of them (with Carol a few paces behind Billy) walked down the road for a while. But because of Billy's lameness, they were both walking very slowly.

Billy finally stopped and turned around.

"Listen. I'm gonna let you carry one of these two pieces..."

He handed one of the two pieces of the scooter to Carol, who happily accepted it.

"...not because I need to but because my ma will be upset if I get home too late."

The two of them now walked down the road side by side.

"How'd you hurt your leg?" Carol asked innocently.

"I forgot," answered Billy. "You're new in town. It wasn't my fault. I got thrown by a horse. My ma and pa didn't have enough money to get it fixed right."

"When did it happen?" asked Carol innocently.

Billy stopped and turned to face her.

"Look. I don't want to talk about it, OK?"

"OK," said Carol. "I'm sorry if I said something that upset you."

"You've got a lot to learn," commented Billy glumly.

They continued walking down the country road.

After a while, Billy and Carol arrived in front of his family farm.

There was a ramshackle farmhouse that had seen better days and a barn and a corral. There was also an "out building" that has been converted into living quarters for his grandmother, Bess.

"Here's where I get off," announced Billy.

"You live here with your folks?"

"Nah. With my ma and my grandma. She's a sidekick!" he said proudly.

"A what?"

"A sidekick. She can see the future. She even knows when I'm coming to see her before I do."

Carol handed Billy the piece of his scooter that she had been carrying.

"I hope you'll be OK, Billy," said Carol.

Billy turned to enter the gate in front of his house and with his back to her said, "Don't worry 'bout me. I can take care of myself."

Carol watched as he placed the two pieces of his scooter by the front door and then entered his house.

Then Carol shook her head, turned and walked away.

Billy, black eye, torn and bloodied clothes and all, entered the house.

His mother had already returned from the Bartletts' house. She was lean and about thirty-five years old but looked older. However, she was still attractive.

Because he had had to limp home rather than use his scooter, Billy was later than usual, and his mother was worried about him. And when she saw the way he looked, with his torn clothes, black eye, and blood on his hair, she became even more upset.

"Oh, my, Billy, whatever happened to you!"

She rushed over to inspect his face.

"Nuthin', Ma. Jess some roughhousin' with t'other boys is all."

"Just a minute," said Diane and then she rushed into the kitchen.

Billy put down the papers that he had in his pocket.

Diane returned with a damp napkin and tried to wipe his face with it, but Billy pulled away from her and walked away.

"I told you — I'm all right," said Billy.

Diane asked, "Which boys was it?", but Billy just said, "I gotta fix somethin'," and walked out the front door.

Outside, Billy picked up the two pieces of his scooter and started to carry them towards the barn.

Diane, now standing in the doorway, called out after him.

"You got to be more careful, Billy. After losin' your pa, I can't afford to lose you, too!"

About a half hour later, Billy was walking from the barn past the house with the now-fixed scooter in his hands when he peeked into a side window of his house. There he saw his mother seated and bent over some papers that were spread out on the table in front of her. She looked like she had been crying.

Billy put his scooter next to the front door. He knew she would be embarrassed if he caught her like that, so he made sure to make some extra noise as he climbed up the wooden steps of the front porch and opened the screen door.

His mother had dried her cheeks by the time he entered, but she still looked sad and worried. She got up and went into the living room where Billy has just entered.

"D'ja get your scooter fixed, Billy?" Diane asked.

"Good as new," Billy replied confidently.

"You always was a handy fella," Diane responded. "Just like your pa..."

But her voice trailed off in sad memories and her eyes started to get moist again.

Then, continuing: "Well, go get ready for dinner. It's almost time."

A few minutes later, Bess came in to join them. She was Billy's father's mother and was about seventy years old. No matter how busy she was with her farm chores, Grandma Bess always found the time to talk (and listen) to Billy.

The only problem was that she was also a little peculiar. That is, she thought she could communicate with all sorts of ghosts and gods and saints, just like they were sitting in her living room talking with her. She especially liked to talk to the Greek gods.

After they set the table, they all sat down, and Diane said grace.

"...And thank you for all our blessings and good fortune."

But when Billy looked over at Bess, she winked at him, making him smile.

"Amen," Diane concluded.

Then they all started to serve themselves from the serving plates in the middle of the table. The food in one dish was unfamiliar to Billy.

"What's this?" asked Billy.

"That's called 'succotash,'" Diane answered. "You don't have to try it if you don't want to."

"Why don't you try it, Billy?" Bess prodded. "You might like it."

"I said, he don't have to try it if he don't want to!" said Diane, annoyed.

Bess made a face as Billy pushed the bowl of succotash away.

Diane looked at Bess. "I don't know why you insist on staying in that old shed. You could move back in here, you know."

"Oh, it ain't so bad," responded Bess as she looked conspiratorially at Billy.

"Besides, it's closer to the outhouse," she said, winking at him again.

Billy laughed at the joke.

"I don't know how you can be making jokes at a time like this," scolded Diane.

"I guess it's because I'm not as worried as you are," said Bess as she helped herself to some of the succotash. "I have faith that the gods will take care of everything."

This comment angered Diane, who crossed herself and then yelled at Bess.

"Bess Diangelo, you should know better than to make such a blasphemous comment in this house! There is only one God, and I won't have you filling Billy's mind with such nonsense!"

"Billy can take care of himself," responded Bess.

"Just remember," countered Diane, "that he's my son and I'll decide how he'll be raised."

"At least Jed trusted me to do what's right," Bess said as she chewed. "As Apollo was telling me the other day..."

With that, Diane stood up.

"That's it!" she exploded. "I asked you politely not to talk about your Greek gods, and now I'm gonna ask you politely to take your food and eat in your shed."

"All right, all right," said Bess as she stood up, picked up her plate of food and started to leave. But before she did, she turned back to Diane.

"There's just one thing I don't understand. If you believe in your god with all you heart, why don't you trust Him more?"

With that, Bess turned and left.

Diane sat back down and tried to calm down.

"Ma, why can't you and Grandma Bess get along?" asked Billy.

"She's not in touch with reality, that's why. She still believes in Saturday matinee dreams that everything will turn out OK just by wishin' it. But the only thing that matters in this country anymore is money — as in dollars and cents."

Diane got up.

"And I don't want you spendin' too much time with her. She's not right in the head."

Diane turned and entered the kitchen, leaving Billy to finish his dinner alone.

The next day, Hector — their Mexican-American farm hand (about fifty-years-old) — and Diane were picking corn. The stalks were short and brown.

The hot sun was shining down relentlessly, but Hector was wearing a sombrero.

Hector was working at a normal pace and was sweating profusely, but Diane was working at breakneck speed and was sweating even more than Hector was.

Hector paused, took off his neckerchief and used it to wipe the sweat from his face. This angered Diane.

"We'll never get this done if you stop to take a break every five minutes!" Diane chided him.

"Senora, it doesn't matter how fast we work — the corn is no good."

Hector opened one of the ears of corn to show Diane what was inside: a small misshapen cob with few kernels of corn on it.

Hector looked at her and shook his head.

Diane looked off in the distance. Then she looked down at the corn cobs she had already picked.

Finally, she dropped the bag of corn cobs she was holding and then walked away.

The next morning, Billy and Diane were in the back seat of a horse-drawn carriage. Hector was seated in the front seat "driving" the horse.

Diane yelled out to Bess, who was working in a small garden patch near her shed: "We're goin' into town ta pay the mortgage and get some things. Be back soon."

Bess looked up. "All right. Say hello to Axton for me!"

Diane made a face, and then said to Hector, "Let's go."

Hector snapped the reins and they were on their way.

When Billy, Diane and Hector arrived in town, Hector "parked" the carriage in front of the bank. They found Rufus seated holding a half-full bottle of beer on the walkway next to front door of the bank. He was a gentle man but he had a drinking problem.

"We won't be long, Hector," advised Diane. "C'mon Billy."

When Diane and Billy got out of the carriage, Rufus greeted them.

"Mornin', Miss Diangelo," he said in a drunken slur.

"Hello, Rufus," Diane said kindly. "How's your family?"

"Fine, thank you," he replied.

"Well, they wouldn't be too happy if they knew you're drinking away the rent money," scolded Diane.

And with that, Diane went over and took the half-full bottle of beer out of his hand and poured it out on the ground.

"Now, why'd you have to go and do that, Miss Diangelo?" Rufus protested. "That was gonna be my last bottle —I swear."

"It's for your own good, Rufus," said Diane as she and Billy entered the bank.

As soon as she entered the bank, Diane took an envelope out of her purse.

"You wait here, Billy. I have to give this to Mr. Bartlett."

Mr. Bartlett was seated in a windowed office at the back of the bank. About fifty years old, he was somewhat overweight — he indeed was shaped like a pear — and balding. He wore business suits that seemed a little too small for his expanding body. In the small town where they lived, he was a "big fish in a small pond." He had a hard time pretending to be warm and friendly.

Diane walked to the back of the bank and motioned to Mr. Bartlett through the glass. When Mr. Bartlett saw her, he smiled and motioned for her to come in.

But Billy did not stay at the front of the bank as he was told to do — he went to the back of the bank to observe the conversation between Diane and Mr. Bartlett. And this is what he saw through the glass:

Diane said something to Mr. Bartlett and handed him the envelope. But instead of taking money *out of it*, Mr. Bartlett put some money *into it* and then handed it back to Diane. And after she took the envelope back from him and put it away, Mr. Bartlett took her hand in his hand.

Billy was shocked to see this.

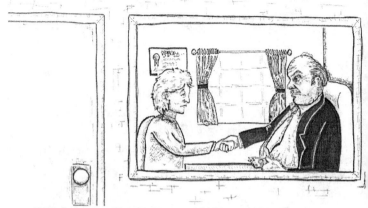

When Mr. Bartlett realized that Billy was watching them, he quickly pulled his hand back. Then Diane turned and also realized that Billy had been watching them, so she blushed and stood up and quickly exited his "office."

Mr. Bartlett stood up and followed her out.

"Billy, I thought I told you...," Diane began, but Mr. Bartlett interrupted her.

"Well, hello there, William. I hear from my Arthur that you and he got into a bit of a dustup t'other day."

"T'weren't nuthin'. Just a little dis'greement, s'all," replied Billy in a dull monotone.

Diane formally shook Mr. Bartlett's hand.

"Well, thank you for everything, Mr. Bartlett."

"Don't mention it," replied Mr. Bartlett. "And say hello to Bess for me."

"I will, Mr. Bartlett," Diane said.

She walked over to Billy and took his arm...

"C'mon, Billy."

...and practically dragged him to the front of the bank.

"I thought I told you to stay in the front of the bank!" she said sternly.

"I'm sorry, Ma," replied Billy.

"Just remember — you can't always believe what you see."

Diane and Billy exited the bank followed by Mr. Bartlett.

Diane and Billy get in the carriage.

"OK, Hector, let's go," Diane said.

Hector flicked the reins and the carriage pulled away.

"Bye, now!" called out Mr. Bartlett in his phony way.

Then Mr. Bartlett turned to re-enter the bank but he was met by Rufus.

"Say Mr. Banker, ah, I mean, Mr. Bartlett... Could ya spare a dime for a good cause?

"A good cause, huh?" replied Mr. Bartlett angrily. "Listen, you drunk — if you don't get away from my bank and stay away, I'll give you a good cause to go to jail!

And with that, he re-entered the bank.

On another street in town, the carriage with Diane, Billy and Hector in it pulled up in front of Axton Twilly's store.

"Now you stay here with Hector," Diane told Billy. "I don't want you gettin' into any trouble this time."

"Yes, Ma," replied Billy.

Diane went into the store.

Axton was setting up a display. He was a kind man around forty years old— the strong silent "Western" type. He had never married. He had long been smitten with Diane but he was still too shy to come right out and say it after her husband died.

When Axton saw that Diane has entered, he awkwardly stood up.

"Well, hello, Diane. How are things?" he said, smiling.

"Same as always, I guess."

"What can I do for you?"

"Let's see..."

She looked around at what was on display.

"I'll take a sack of potatoes, a bag of flour, a pound of lima beans... oh, and you'd better get me some sewing thread — brown."

Axton spoke to her as he went to get what she asked for.

"You know, we don't hardly see you in town anymore, least not often enough."

"Things are busy at the farm," Diane explained. "The harvest and all."

By now Axton had assembled what she asked for.

"That'll be a dollar forty-nine. I can put it on your account, if you want," he offered.

But Diane pulled out the envelope and took two five-dollar bills from it.

"Here you are," she said, handing the bills to Axton.

"But these are two fives," he said, surprised.

"That's for what I already owe you."

"You don't have to do that — I know you're good for it.

"I just want to even up all my accounts, is all," said Diane seriously.

Axton frowned and then sighed as he put the money away.

"All right, Diane. Whatever you say."

After Axton had finished loading the stuff Diane had purchased into the carriage, the carriage pulled away. Billy turned around to wave at Axton, who waved back, but Diane stayed facing forward.

Axton: "Bye, now!"

Billy: "Bye, Mr. Twilly!"

After Billy turned back to face forward, he looked into Diane's face to try to discern what she was thinking, but she just kept looking ahead with a stern expression on her face.

Meanwhile, Axton, with a disappointed expression on his face, turned and re-entered his store.

On the way home from their trip into town, there was suddenly something odd about the weather. Even though the sky was clear, little gusts of wind were bursting around them. Then, off in the distance, a strange cloud appeared. It was gold-colored and it was moving at a fast pace not too far off the ground, almost like a weak egg-shaped tornado.

Hector was the first one to notice it.

"Will you look at that!"

Diane and Billy looked off towards where Hector was looking.

"That's the strangest tornado I ever saw!" Hector continued.

The wind around them got stronger, and the strange cloud seemed to be moving straight towards their farm.

"Hector!" Diane cried. "Bess is home alone!"

Hector snapped the reins and the horse headed home at a faster pace.

When they came up over a rise, they realized that the strange gold tornado-like cloud was setting down right at their farm!

Hector gave the reins another snap and now they were flying home as fast as the horse would take them.

But just as they approached their farm, the strange gold cloud lifted off the ground and quickly moved away.

By the time they got home, everything seemed perfectly normal. Not even a leaf had been blown away.

Diane quickly got out of the carriage to check on Bess, but as she approached Bess's shed, Bess came out of it, even more calm and serene than usual.

"Are you OK?" asked Diane, excited.

"Hmm?" Bess replied. "Oh, you mean the cloud? It was beautiful, wasn't it?" she said serenely.

"Then everything is all right here?" Diane asked.

"Yes, of course," replied Bess.

Diane sighed a sigh of relief but looked around, puzzled.

"I was just worried," she said.

Then, just as Diane turned to leave, Bess said, "Oh, by the way, while you were gone, someone — an old friend — was here."

Diane looked over to where Bess was looking, at the corral. In it was a broken-down old horse.

"He owed me some money," Bess continued, "but I let him leave a horse instead."

Billy stared at the horse with fear on his face.

Diane angrily turned to Bess.

"Bess, you know what our financial situation is! We could have used that money. And how do you expect us to pay for his upkeep?"

"I'm sure we'll find a way, somehow," Bess replied.

Diane scowled at Bess and then turned to go help unload the carriage.

"C'mon, Billy. Let's take the stuff in."

Bess, however, had a heavenly contented smile on her face.

That afternoon, Diane was seated on the sofa in the living room, darning some socks with the thread she had bought earlier in the day when Billy came in.

"Ma, I was just wondering..."

Diane looked up. "Hmm?"

"About the bank..."

"I thought I told you to forget about that," Diane scolded him.

Billy was disappointed and started to leave, but, after thinking about it for a moment, Diane called him back:

"Billy, c'min here."

Billy walked into the living room where Diane was seated. Her eyes started to moisten and she looked away from Billy.

"Listen, Billy. I got somethin' 'portant to talk to you about. It's about, well, it's about our future."

Billy slipped nervously into the big green upholstered chair.

"What is it, Momma?" Billy asked somberly.

"It's like this, Billy," Diane began. "You know we've been having some hard times since your pa died. First, there was your doctor bills. Then I had to pay for your pa's funeral. Then I needed money for seed. So I went and convinced your Grandma Bess to take out a mortgage on the farm, and I promised to pay it back for her."

Diane stood up, walked over and knelt in front of Billy and took his hands in hers.

"Billy, you're a big boy now so it's time I told you the truth, but I want you to swear to God that you won't tell Grandma."

"I swear, Momma," said Billy, worried.

Diane stood up, walked over and looked out a window.

"Times is bad, Billy. I did my best, but with the drought and all, I haven't always been able to pay the mortgage."

Billy shifted uneasily in his chair.

Diane turned to face Billy again.

"Now, Mr. Bartlett has been kind enough to let me extend it — with interest, of course —

but there's just no way I can put him off much longer."

"So what're we gonna do, Momma?" Billy asked.

"Well, there's only one solution I can think of. Mr. Bartlett said he'd take care of the mortgage if..."

"If what, Momma?"

"If I marry him."

Billy jumped up out of the chair like a jackrabbit that had just been shot at.

"What! With Poppa hardly even dead 'n' buried?"

He stepped towards her.

"You can't marry him, Momma! No, you can't!"

She stepped away from him.

"I'm sorry, son, but I don't see any other way. There's no way I can make enough money to pay off the mortgage, and I won't see you and Grandma Bess homeless.

"Well, if you married him," Billy asked, "could we still live here on the farm?"

Diane slumped into the chair.

"I'm afraid not, Billy. The farm would be sold. I'd move in with Mr. Bartlett.

"But, Momma — that would mean I'd have to live in the same house with Arthur! And what would happen to Grandma Bess and Hector?"

Diane stood up again, walked over to the window and gazed out it.

"Hector will have to take care of himself. Billy, there's somethin' else I gotta tell you..."

She gathered her strength and then turned back towards him.

"With the money from the sale, Grandma Bess could be put in an old people's home. But..."

She inhaled and then sighed.

"But Mr. Bartlett made it a condition of our marriage that you go away to boarding school."

"What!" Billy cried out frantically.

He limped over to where Diane was standing, got down on his knees, and put his tear-dampened cheek to her dress.

"No, Momma," he whimpered. "Please don't send me away! I'll do anything! Please, oh please, don't send me away, Momma!"

She pulled away from him, walked over to the table and picked up a handkerchief that was lying there.

"I'm sorry, Billy, but Mr. Bartlett says it's what best for you. He says he knows a school where they take care of..."

She swallowed hard.

"Cripples?" said Billy. "Is that you was goin' to say?"

She turned away and wiped her eyes with the handkerchief.

"I'm sorry, Billy. But Mr. Bartlett said...

Billy took a couple steps toward her.

"I don't care what Mr. Bartlett says!" Billy said, now crying. "I'm not goin' away to school, and I'm not gonna let him marry you!"

Diane turned to try to reason with him but Billy was already going out the door.

Diane sat down, put her faces in her hands, and started to sob.

Out front, Billy saw Hector fixing some farm equipment.

"Hector, is my grandma around?"

Hector motioned with his head and eyes towards her shed.

"She's in there. But she may be having one of her seances..."

"Thanks, Hector," said Billy, and then he went up to an open window of the shed where he could hear Bess talking to someone.

"That sounds like a good plan," Bess was saying.

Billy peeked in and saw Bess seated alone, talking to nobody.

"And it just may work," she continued.

Billy stood in front of Bess's shed, trying to decide whether to knock on the door.

But before he did anything, Bess opened the front door.

"Hi, Billy. I been expecting you."

Billy went inside.

Despite the fact that it was just a one-room shed, Bess had decorated it nicely so it had a comfy feeling. There was a bed and a table and drawings of Greek gods on the walls.

Bess gave him some milk to drink and then sat down and started knitting, but Billy put down the glass, stood up and started to pace.

"What am I gonna do, Grandma? I don't wanna go away to boarding school!"

He turned back to face her. "Can't I stay here with you?"

"That would be fine with me, Billy," said Bess, "but you know I haven't been in the best of health, lately. What would happen if I got sick?"

Billy got down on his knees and put his hands on Bess's knees.

"I'll help you if you get sick, Gran'ma. And me and Hector kin run the farm. I know how to do everything."

Bess smiled at Billy's earnestness. Then she stood up and walked over and gazed out the window.

"Billy, dear, you remember that horse that someone gave me?"

Billy walked up and stood beside her and looked out the window.

The horse was standing in the corral.

Bess turned to talk to Billy, who continued to stare out the window.

"Her name is 'Peggy.' She doesn't belong to me, Billy. Someone just left her with me."

Bess walked away from the window.

"The problem is that she's no use to me the way she is."

She turned back towards Billy.

"You see, Billy, she's afraid of people. If you want to show me what you can do around here, you can start by seeing what you can do with her."

Billy turned away from the window and faced Bess.

"Well, what do you want me to do with her?" asked Billy, worried.

"Just see if you can help her get over her jitters, that's all. She's either got to be broken and made to do some useful work or I'll have to find some way to return her.

"Either that," she continued, ominously, "or I'll have to put her down."

Billy looked seriously at Bess a moment and then turned around to look out at Peggy again. He stared out at the horse with an expression of fear on his face.

Billy had been afraid of horses ever since the accident when one threw him, breaking his leg. His parents didn't have the money to pay for proper medical care, so they just had to let his leg bones and knee grow back together as best they could. That's why Billy's right leg was as stiff as a board.

Later that day, Billy was standing with his right foot on the lowest rail of the fence around the corral. He and Peggy were sizing each other up.

Hector was working on something nearby.

"She sure is one ugly hoss," opined Billy.

Hector realized that Billy was talking to him and came over alongside Billy to admire Peggy with him.

"She sure is, ain't she? I never seen one like her, least not in these parts."

"Grandma says nobody's been able to ride her."

"I tried to ride her myself," said Hector, "but she just wouldn't let me. Never seen a horse so strong and ornery and independent, all in one."

"Dya think it's safe to go in the corral with her?" asked Billy, worried.

"I wouldn't try it if I was you," advised Hector. "I mean, with your bad leg and all, you might not be able to get away if she came at you."

Billy turned and started to walk away from the corral.

"Well, then, this don't make no sense at all," said Billy, relieved. "I'll just go tell Grandma to forget the whole thing."

Billy started to walk back toward Bess's shed.

But then Bill stopped and turned to look back at Peggy, who was staring at Billy, so they just stared at each other for a few moments.

And in that moment when their gazes met, Billy knew that Peggy was keeping something dark and heavy in her heart, like the dark and heavy thing that he had been carrying around in his heart ever since his accident and his father died, something so dark and heavy that it was weighing both of them down. And he knew at that moment that it was finally time to stop using his injury as an excuse to avoid challenges.

And his grandmother, looking out from between the curtains in her front window, smiled, for she also knew that, at that moment, Peggy, Billy and she all needed each other, and that from that day onward none of their lives would ever be the same.

She also knew something about Peggy that she hadn't told anybody. But she wasn't about to reveal that secret... at least not yet.

The next morning, Billy was making his way with some difficulty to a bank overlooking the creek.

He settled down on the bank. As he looked up at the clouds, he started to think back to the last time he rode a horse...

Two years earlier, Billy had been riding a horse while his father Jed split some logs near the barn...

The horse reared up, but the ten-year-old Billy managed to hold on.

His father looked up from his work.

"You best be careful, Billy. Betty can be wild if you mistreat her."

"I can handle her, Pa. Don't worry."

"Just be careful. Don't do anything stupid while I'm inside."

"I won't, Pa."

His father went in the house, and Billy spoke to Betty:

"C'mon, girl. Let's show 'em what we can do!"

Billy rode a little distance away from the fence and then turned the horse around. He dug his heels into the sides of the horse and said, "Let's go!"

Then he headed for the fence.

They went faster and faster and faster.

Just then, Diane came out the front door of the house. When she saw what was happening, she freaked out and screamed.

"Billy, what are you doing!"

Perhaps because of her scream, the horse pulled up just before they got to the fence. Billy flew though the air and did a somersault before he landed hard against a fence post.

"Oh, my God!" screamed Diane. Then to Jed, inside the house:

"Jed, come quick!"

Diane ran over to where Billy was lying crumpled on the ground, holding his right leg.

She knelt down beside him and said, "Billy, are you all right?"

Billy just looked up at her and groaned, "Oooohhh."

By now Jed had arrived and he too knelt next to Billy.

"You all right, son?..."

Just then, Billy heard Carol's voice.

"Billy, are you all right?"

Billy, startled, opened his eyes and saw Carol standing over him.

"Are you all right?" Carol repeated.

Billy scrambled to his feet.

"What are you doing here?"

"Your grandmother told me you might be here," Carol explained.

Billy was surprised to hear this news.

"My grandma? She don't know about this place."

"Well, she does now," Carol said firmly.

Billy walked a few steps away from Carol, picked up some stones and started to skip them in the creek.

"Well, what do you want?" he said in a sour voice.

"I was just worried about you, after the fight and all. And I was wondering how you're doin'.

"I'm doin' fine," said Billy in an unfriendly way.

Then he looked up at the sky and got a surprised expression on his face for in the sky was a cloud that looks amazingly like a horse.

"Well, whaddaya gonna do this summer?" Carol asked.

"I'm not sure," Billy said. "My grandma wants me to train her horse, but..."

Billy turned around and started to walk quickly back towards the lane. Carol followed close after him.

"But what?" asked Carol.

"But I gotta get home now."

On the way home on the country lane, Billy pushed his scooter slow enough for Carol to keep up with him — she was just a step or two behind him.

"At least you have one parent," began Carol. "I live with my aunt and uncle."

Billy was interested to hear this.

"What happened to your ma and pa?" he said without looking at her.

"My dad left when I was three," Carol explained. "And then my ma got sick and passed away.

"I don't even have a bicycle," she said sadly.

They continued on in silence for a moment. Then Billy stopped, stepped off his scooter, and turned towards her.

"Listen! How'd you like a scooter like this one? I can make one up for ya, if ya like."

Carol was overjoyed to hear this.

"Really? Sure — that would be great!"

Billy got back on his scooter and continued down the road, but now he went slow enough so Carol could walk beside him. He also had the beginnings of a smile on his face.

When they arrived back at the Diangelo home, an expensive new 1935 car was parked in front of the house.

"Listen, I gotta go," said Billy, eyeing the car warily.

"OK, Billy," said Carol. "But don't forget about my scooter! Bye!"

"Bye."

After Carol left, Billy walked over to where Bess was working in her garden.

"Hi, Grandma!"

She looked up at him.

"Oh, hi, Billy!" She looked over at the car. "Looks like Mr. Bartlett is here."

"Yeah," said Billy with a sour expression on his face. "I guess he had to talk to Ma about the mortgage."

"Well, whatever happens is fine with me," said Bess, looking down.

Billy's tone lightened a bit.

"Grandma — about the horse. I been thinking."

"Yes?" said Bess, looking up at him.

"I been thinking that... I wanna think about it some more."

"That's OK," said Bess, getting back to her gardening. "Take your time. The paths of our lives are woven by the Fates. You just have to discover what your life path is."

Billy walked up in front of the house and then paused a moment to gather himself.

Then, he climbed up the steps and entered the house.

Inside the house, Mr. Bartlett and Diane were seated at the dining room table going over the papers which were spread out there. When Billy entered, Mr. Bartlett stood up formally.

"Hello, William," said Mr. Bartlett.

"Hello, Mr. Bartlett," offered Billy, coldly.

Billy walked past the two of them and into the kitchen. Diane called after him:

"I heard you talkin' to Grandma."

"Uh-huh," said Billy from the kitchen.

"I thought I told you not to spend so much time with her."

Billy reappeared from the kitchen with a partly-eaten apple in his hand.

"She's all right," he said between bites into the apple. "She's nice to me. And she wants me to take care of her horse Peggy this summer.

Hearing this, Mr. Bartlett exploded in laughter.

"Peggy! That old nag! I've seen her. The only thing she is good for is a glue factory."

Hearing this, Billy exploded in anger.

"I bet she's got more of a heart than you'll ever have!"

Shocked by Billy's rudeness, Diane stood up.

"Don't you talk that way to your future stepfather, boy, or I'll take a switch to your behind!"

By now, Billy was almost hysterical.

"Well, I don't want him to be my stepfather or my anything-else-father, for that matter!"

"Well, I'm afraid you'll just have to get used to it," declared Diane.

"And then you ship me out to the home for cripples?" cried Billy.

"Now, William," Mr. Bartlett intervened, "you shouldn't think of it like that. They have a special curriculum and special facilities for children like you. You'll like it, once you get used to it."

"Well, I ain't goin' — nowhere, no how, no way, never!

And with that, Billy went into his bedroom and partially closed the door behind him and sat down on his bed.

Diane sat back down and let out a big sigh.

"I just hope we're doin' what's best for him."

Mr. Bartlett walked around behind her and awkwardly leaned over and put his arms around her.

"Don't worry — I'll take care of everything," he said, half comforting, half ominously.

From his bedroom, Billy could hear the conversation from the other room.

"It's getting late. I better be going," said Mr. Bartlett.

"So you want to wait until after the Labor Day race, then?" asked Diane.

"Yes. It's gonna be the biggest steeplechase race in the history of the county. In fact, I'm going to put up $500 of the bank's money as first prize."

When Billy heard this, he perked up considerably. He got off the bed and walked over to the door.

"But you know Arthur is bound to win," Diane protested. "He's the best rider in the country."

"All the better!" chortled Mr. Bartlet.

Through the crack in his door, Billy saw Mr. Bartlett with his hat in his hands standing by the front door, which Diane was holding open for him.

"And then we get married," continued Mr. Bartlett.

"That's right, Mr. Bartlett," said Diane.

"Now, Didi. Don't you think it's time you started calling me 'Phil'?"

With some difficulty, Diane managed to mouth the word.

"All right... 'Phil.'"

Mr. Bartlett leaned over and gave Diane a peck on the check.

Watching them from his bedroom, Billy grimaced.

Mr. Bartlett started to leave.

"Bye, Didi."

"Goodbye...," said Diane as she closed the door behind him, "Mr. Bartlett."

Diane headed for the kitchen but she was cut off by Billy.

"Momma, that's it!" exclaimed Billy.

"What are you talking about?" said Diane as she pushed past him and walked into the kitchen with Billy following close behind.

"How much money would it take to pay off the mortgage on the farm?" he asked, excited.

"Why, about $400, I think," said Diane. "Why? Are you fixin' to rob a bank or somethin'?"

"No, Momma. I'm gonna get it fair and square!"

"And just how do you propose to do that?" asked Diane.

Diane tried to start preparing dinner, but Billy kept getting in her way. Finally, Billy forced her to stop what she was doing and look at him.

"I'm gonna win the steeplechase, Momma! Mr. Bartlett said there's a five hunnerd dollar prize. That's enough to pay off the mortgage!"

Diane pulled away from him and returned to the task of fixing dinner.

"Why that's the most ridiculous thing I ever heard! You expect to beat Arthur Bartlett, the best rider in the county, when you never even been in a race before?"

"I know I kin do it, Ma!" pleaded Billy.

"And the way Mr. Bartlett tells it," Diane continued, "that horse ain't worth a plug nickel.

"No, I absolutely forbid it! You stay away from that horse. You almost got killed once on a horse, and that's enough for this lifetime."

Billy was speechless.

Later that day, Billy tried to give some feed to Peggy through the fence, but she refused it, and he walked away disappointed.

But then he saw Bess sitting on her porch, knitting and watching him, so he turned around and tried again. And this time when Billy, still scared, gave the feed to Peggy through the fence, she accepted it.

Billy smiled a half smile.

Just then, Carol walked up to the front of the Diangelo home and knocked on the front door.

"Hello? Billy? Anyone home?"

Billy appeared from around the corner.

"Hi!"

"Oh, hi! I got your message," said Carol.

"C'mon 'round here," said Billy as he headed back around the corner of the house.

Billy entered the barn followed closely behind by Carol.

"Over here," he said over his shoulder.

Billy stepped behind a workbench and pulled out a wooden scooter, which he presented to Carol.

"I made it for you," said Billy proudly.

Carol was overwhelmed.

"Oh, Billy, thank you! It's wonderful!"

She impulsively leaned in to give him a hug and a kiss, but he pushed her away.

"Hey — what are you doing?" he said angrily, wiping her kiss off his cheek.

"I was just trying to thank you, that's all," she replied, confused.

"Just 'cause I made you a scooter don't mean you're my girlfriend," said Billy, shaking his head in disgust.

"Well, maybe I'm not even your friend!" said Carol, hurt and angry.

As Carol ran out of the barn, Billy realized that he had not handled the situation well.

Carol, upset, walked past the Diangelo home and started to walk down the road, but Billy came after her on his scooter while managing to carry the scooter he made for her under his arm.

"Hey, where you goin'?" asked Billy as he caught up to her.

"Anywhere," she responded looking straight ahead as she continued to walk.

"Well, wouldn't it be easier if you did it on a scooter?" asked Billy.

"I don't know," said Carol as she stopped to face him. "Aren't you afraid that I might try to kiss you again."

"Not so much," said Billy this time.

Carol considered the situation for a moment and then reached out to receive the scooter. He moved closer to her to give her the scooter and then stood there after she took it from him. Then he looked down.

She tentatively moved closer to him and then gently planted a kiss on his cheek.

He smiled and then hopped on his scooter and pushed about ten yards out in front of her.

"C'mon!" he yelled. "Let's go to town! My grandma gave me some money."

"I don't know, Billy..." answered Carol.

"C'mon! I'll buy you a soda!" said Billy enticingly.

Convinced, Carol smiled, hopped on her scooter and pushed up to where he was.

"Let's go!" she said.

They happily pushed down the road together towards town.

When they reached town, Carol and Billy pulled up in front of Axton's store and dismounted.

"You watch our scooters," Billy said to Carol. "I'll be right out."

And with that, Billy entered the store.

Axton was behind the counter when Billy entered.

"Hello, Mr. Twilly!" said Billy brightly.

"Well, hello, Billy," Axton said, happy to see him. "What can I do for ya?"

"Two sodas, please!" Billy responded like a big spender.

Axton took two sodas from a cooler and put them on the counter.

"That'll be ten cents," he said.

Billy pulled some change out of his pocket and counted it, but when he realized he doesn't have enough money, his face fell.

"Gee, Mr. Twilly. I don't think I got enough."

"How much do you have?" Axton said, considering the situation.

Billy put a nickel and three pennies on the counter.

Axton picked up the change.

"My gosh, you know what?," he said. "I plum forgot. We got a special on soda today — two for eight cents."

"Thanks, Mr. Twilly!" Billy said, smiling.

Billy eagerly grabbed the two sodas and turned to leave, but before he did, Axton called to him.

"Oh, Billy..."

Billy turned back towards him.

"You give my regards to your ma, OK?"

"OK," said Billy.

Axton smiled at Billy as he left the store.

But when Billy came out of the store, he found Molly and Wally standing there talking to Carol. She looked scared.

"Well, if it tain't that little cripple boy," snarled Molly.

"We was just asking your little girlfriend here if she'd like to take a ride with us some time," added Wally.

Billy handed one soda to Carol and took his scooter from her.

"C'mon, Carol. We don't have to waste our time talking to these no-accounts."

Axton appeared at the window to see what all the commotion was about.

Holding his soda, Billy started to leave on his scooter and Carol, holding her soda, followed him on her scooter.

"Bye, scooter boy!" Molly taunted him. "Don't fall off and hurt yourself!"

Molly and Wally both cackled at what Molly had said.

Axton was now standing in the doorway with a broom in his hand.

"You two boys fixin' to buy something?" he asked them.

"No, sir," replied Wally.

"Then git," said Axton sternly. "I gotta sweep the dirt off the porch."

And Axton started sweeping even before Wally and Molly had a chance to move.

On the road home, Carol and Billy were both holding a soda as they pushed their scooters.

But Billy was pushing his scooter so fast that Carol couldn't keep up with him. She called after him:

"Wait up! What's the hurry?"

He stopped abruptly and turned to face her.

"Aren't you afraid to be seen with a coward and a cripple?" he asked, close to tears.

"What are you talking about?" replied Carol. "You mean those two fools back in town?"

When Billy turned away from her so she won't see his moist eyes, Carol understood that that was precisely why he was upset.

She got off her scooter and walked over to him.

"Listen," she said. "It doesn't matter how you get somewhere. The only thing that matters is that you do get there."

He still wouldn't look at her.

She got an idea.

"Hey, you know what? We haven't even drunk our sodas yet. Bet you I can finish first!"

Hearing this, Billy's mood lightened and he turned back towards her.

"Bet chu can't!" he said.

They laughingly had a contest to see who could drink their sodas first. The bubbly liquid made them giggle even more.

Some time later, Billy and Carol were silently pushing along the country road on their scooters. They stopped when they come to a crossroads.

"Well, it's getting late," said Billy somberly. "You best be leaving now if you wanna get home before dark."

Carol was also sad to see the most wonderful day in her life about to end.

"Thanks for the soda, Billy. And for the scooter."

"S'all right," offered Billy.

She turned to leave, and so did he, but then she turned back to speak to Billy:

"And Billy..."

He turned back towards her.

"Yes?"

"Don't worry — you'll get where you're goin'. I know you will."

"Thanks," said Billy.

Then he walked over and gave her a kiss on the cheek.

They exchanged a loving glance.

"Bye," said Carol.

"Bye," said Billy.

She turned, got on her scooter, and, with a big smile on her face, started down the road.

Billy watched her go for a minute with a smile on his face. Then he turned, got on his scooter, and set off down another road as he yelled a big "Yahoo!"

When Billy arrived back home on his scooter, he went over to the corral and leerily stared at Peggy.

Bess, dressed to go to town, walked up beside him.

"What's wrong, Billy?" Bess asked. "You look like a goat who just swallowed a shoe."

"I'm still scared of her, Grandma."

"Just believe in yourself, Billy," Bess said tenderly. "And have the faith that things will work out.

Just then, Didi drove up in the carriage.

Bess continued: "Now Didi and I are going to town. Maybe while we're away, you and Peggy could try to get better acquainted."

She winked at Billy and then got in the carriage.

"We'll be back in a couple hours, Billy," Diane called out.

After Diane and Bess left, Billy turned to look at Peggy standing in the corral.

Billy carefully opened the gate and let himself into the corral. He almost completely closed the gate behind him but left a small gap to allow him to escape, if necessary.

Peggy whinnied and pulled back to the far side of the corral.

Taking one small step with his good left foot and dragging his stiff right foot up to meet it, Billy tentatively walked across the corral.

"You don't have to be afraid of me, girl. You know I'd never hurt you."

But Peggy kept whinnying as if she was being stalked by a wolf.

Billy stopped halfway across the corral.

"What made you so 'fraid of people, Peg?"

Peggy turned and brushed up against the fence, and, in doing, so she scraped her leg against a nail head that was sticking out of a post. Blood started to trickle down her leg.

"Oh, my goodness, Peg. Now look what you done! Let me take a look at that."

Billy carefully started to move toward her again, and now she didn't seem as eager to get away from him as she had before.

But just as he was close enough to actually reach out and touch her, she bolted past him, knocking him down.

Billy, now on the ground, was hurt and angry at the same time.

"Dammit, Peg, if you don't want anyone to help you, then you can just go to the glue factory, for all I care."

Because of his bad leg, Billy had some trouble getting to his feet, and after he stood up, he started to hobble back to the entrance to the corral.

Billy was just reaching out to open the gate of the corral when he felt something strange on the side of his head. He reacted by pulling back and turning around quickly, only to find that

Peggy was trying to "kiss" him on the side of the head!

When Billy realized what has just happened, he gave Peggy a big hug, and this time she didn't try to pull away.

Billy had tears of joy in his eyes.

"I knew you'd come around! You just had to get to know me, is all."

That evening in the dining room of the Diangelo home, Billy, Diane and Bess were seated, serving themselves dinner.

Billy noticed a bowl of succotash on the table.

"Would you pass that to me, please," Billy asked his mother.

"That's the succotash. You don't eat that," she snapped.

"I just thought I'd try it," said Billy as he reached for and served some to himself, surprising Diane.

"OK," said Diane, "but don't blame me if you don't like it."

"Umm... Not bad," said Billy with his mouth full of succotash.

Bess tried to hide a smile from Diane.

Then Billy continued:

"Ma, I know you don't want me riding Peggy, but it's all right if I try to tame her, isn't it? I mean, I got nothing else to do this summer."

Diane gave a dirty look to Bess and then sighed.

"All right, Billy. I'm no match for the two of you. But you be careful, all right?"

"I will, Ma! I will!" said Billy happily.

Bess tried to hide another smile from Diane.

The next day, Billy, wearing a neckerchief, walked out of the barn with a harness over his shoulder. He picked up some feed, carried it into the corral where Peggy was standing, and gave it to her.

Next, he got a bucket of water and carried it to the corral.

As Peggy stood watching him, he poured out the water from the bucket to wet the dirt in the corral more.

The dirt in the corral was so wet that it was almost mud.

Next, Billy tied the harness securely to a strong fence post. Then he went over to Peggy and took off the neckerchief he was wearing.

"Now, Peg, you gotta trust me on this," he said to her gently.

He put the neckerchief around her head as a blindfold. Then he led her over to where he had previously tied the harness to a fence post.

"Here we go...," he said soothingly. "Nice and easy..."

He slipped the harness over her. Then he took off the handkerchief blindfold and backed away.

At first, Peggy didn't react, but when she started to walk away and realized that she couldn't, she started to whinny and moan and pull and strain on the harness as hard as she could.

Billy and Hector watched from outside the corral as Peggy continued to pull at the harness and whinny in a mournful way.

"It's awful," said Billy.

"But it's the only way, son," replied Hector.

"She'll never trust me again," continued Billy.

"She will, once she knows that you're on her side," Hector said.

After about a half hour, Peggy tired of trying to pull with her head while standing in the slippery mud of the corral, so she stopped resisting and just stood there.

Billy, smiling, untied the harness from the fence and led Peggy from the corral to the barn.

Billy entered his home, excited.

"Ma! Ma! Guess what I got Peggy to do today!"

But there was no response. Billy went over to a calendar hanging on the wall and looked at it.

On the square for July 30, "Mr. Bartlett" was written in Diane's handwriting.

Billy, unhappy, sat down on a sofa in the living room.

Just then, he heard a car pull up outside. He stood up and looked out the window.

Outside, Diane, wearing a brand new dress, was seated next to Mr. Bartlett in his car. They talked for a moment, then he leaned over and gave her a kiss on the cheek. She didn't look eager to accept it, but she did so, stoically.

Seeing this, Billy was filled with a combination of hatred and revulsion.

Diane got out of Mr. Bartlett's car and waved to him as he pulled out. Then she turned and headed for the front door.

When she entered the house, Billy was seated on the sofa in the living room. Diane closed the door behind her and then saw Billy.

"Oh, hi, Billy. I'm sorry I'm late..."

Billy stood up and walked towards her.

"What do you think you're doing?" he demanded.

"What do you mean?" said Diane, taken aback.

"I thought you were marrying Mr. Bartlett because you had to, not because you love him!"

Diane turned away from him to hang up her coat.

"Now, Billy, you'll just have to trust me..."

"Like I trusted you when you made Betty throw me?" said Billy, even angrier. "You don't really care about me or Grandma Bess or the farm."

This hurt Diane deeply. She turned towards him and laid into him.

"Now you listen, young man! One of these days you're going to discover that the world doesn't revolve around you! Now I'm doing the best I can, and if you don't like it..."

"What?" said Billy.

Diane realized that she had let her anger get the best of her.

"You'll just have to learn to live with it, that's all," she said, more calm now.

By now, they were both close to tears. Billy turned away from her and put his hands on the back of a chair.

There was a moment of silence as they both considered what to say next. Then Diane's expression changed from one of anger to one of sympathy and resignation. She walked behind him and put her hands on his shoulders.

"Look — I know I've made some mistakes in my life. A lot of mistakes. But what else can I do, son? You think President Roosevelt is gonna come down from Washington to save us?"

Billy, crying, turned around and embraced her.

"I don't know, Mama. I just wish there was somethin' I could do to help out."

"That's all right, hon," said Diane, looking over his shoulder. "Miracles do happen."

She looked off into the distance.

"They just don't happen in places like this."

Later, as Hector looked on, Billy led Peggy by the harness around the coral for the umpteenth time.

"You got her nice and tame, all right," said Hector. "Don't you think it's time you tried to saddle her up and ride her?"

Billy didn't respond. Instead, he continued to walk Peggy around the corral as he thought about what Hector had said.

"If you'd like, I'll help you break her," Hector offered.

After another couple steps, Billy stopped and addressed Peggy:

"Whadaya say, Peg? You willing to give it a try?"

Peggy responded by licking him on the ear.

The next day, Billy had just finishing giving Peggy a bath, so she was wet. He tied her to a fence post.

He went and picked up an old blanket.

First, he held the blanket in front of Peggy so she could smell it and see what it was. Then he started at the front of her body and worked his way back, so as not to spook her.

Then Billy started to gently slap her with the blanket.

"It's OK, Peg," Billy reassured her. "It's OK."

He started to slap her a little more strongly with the blanket.

"There you go, Peg. There you go," he said reassuringly.

Next, Billy got the bridle and put it over Peggy's head. She complained and whinnied a little bit but soon calmed down.

But when Billy placed the bit in her mouth and untied her, she tore across the corral in an angry fit, almost knocking Billy over as she did so. She reared up and kicked and shook her head, trying to rid herself of the vile piece of metal between her teeth.

Then she looked accusingly at Billy, who was looking on, worried and sympathetic.

"You just gotta trust me, Peg, to know what's best for you."

Peggy finally stopped whinnying and kicking and put her head down.

Billy walked over to her.

"I know it's uncomfortable now, but, in the long run, it's for your own good."

Billy put his arm around her neck and gave her a hug.

Later, Billy was holding Peggy steady as Hector was tying a halter around her left hind leg. Hector pulled Peggy's left hind leg off the ground by tying the other end of the halter around Peggy's neck. Then he stepped back.

"There," he said. "Now she won't be able to kick."

Peggy whinnied in fear and confusion for a few moments but then settled down.

Billy went over, picked up the blanket, and then placed it on her back.

Peggy didn't react, but when Hector helped Billy hoist the saddle on her back, she shied a little and whinnied some more.

While Billy steadied and reassured Peggy — "It's OK, Peg. There you go." — Hector got down and gently tied the girth under her belly. Billy allowed her to look back to see what he was doing.

Hector cinched up the girth even tighter, and finally said, "OK, son. It's time."

Billy backed away as Hector untied the harness.

Peggy started to buck furiously, trying to get rid of the loathsome saddle.

From her shed, Bess was watching the goings-on in the corral with a smile on her face.

Billy and Hector were watching Peggy jump and buck. Hector noticed the worried expression on Billy's face.

"It's all right, son," he said. "It had to be done."

When Peggy finally settled down, Billy appeared with some sugar cubes and fed them to her.

Bess was still watching the goings on in the corral from her shed. She turned her head and, pleased, said to someone:

"It's going just like you said it would."

Then she turned to continue looking out the window.

That night, Billy and Diane were arguing.

"Listen," Diane was saying, "I let you tame her, but that's it — I am not going to let you ride her!"

"But, Ma," Billy pleaded, "how am I gonna win the steeplechase if I don't practice?

"You're not going to win the steeplechase because you're not going to be in the steeplechase! I'm sorry, Billy, but that's my final decision."

Billy stormed into his bedroom and slammed the door behind him.

Later that evening, Diane turned the lights out in the living room and walked over to Billy's bedroom and knocked on his door.

When there was no response, she opened the door a bit and peeked in.

The light was on. Billy was in bed with the covers pulled up to his neck, apparently asleep.

Diane smiled, entered his room, kissed the "sleeping" Billy gently on the forehead, turned off the light, and left.

A few moments later, Billy opened his eyes. Then he pulled back the covers. He was still dressed in the clothes he had been wearing earlier in the day.

Billy exited the front door of the house making as little noise as possible. Luckily, it was a moon-lit night.

He went into the barn.

A few minutes later, Billy led Peggy, all saddled up, out of the barn.

Billy tied Peggy to a fence post in the corral.

Bess pushed the curtain to the side and peered out of her shed.

With great difficulty, Billy climbed up so that, while holding onto Peggy with one hand, he was standing on the top rail. Just then, he started to wobble, as if he was experiencing an earthquake. But when he looked down, he realized it was his body, not the earth, doing the shaking. Despite his best efforts to keep thoughts of his accident hidden in a far recess of his mind, fear was overtaking his body.

He sat back down on the fence rail. Billy wiped some sweat from his brow with the back of his wrist, and said, "Oh, man." This was the first time since the accident that he had had to confront his fear head on, and it was the first time in his life that he had ever had to look at one of his own feelings as an enemy to be fought and defeated.

Bess had a look of concern on her face.

For a moment he considered giving up entirely, but then he saw Peggy standing there patiently, willing to wait as long as it took for him to mount her, and that gave him courage.

Peggy looked back up at him as if to say, "What's the hold up?"

"OK, here we go," he said.

So Billy swallowed his fear and stuck it way down in a corner of his belly where it couldn't do him much harm.

He stood up again on the top rail and, with a mighty sweep, swung his stiff right leg on top of Peggy and over the saddle and pushed his butt into the saddle.

And then... he promptly fell off the other side of the horse!

Bess was startled by what had just happened.

Billy was in a heap on the ground. He slowly crawled to his feet and then shortened the stirrup on Peggy's right side.

"Darn it, Peg. I forgot I couldn't straighten my leg like I used to!"

Billy climbed back up to the top rail of the fence. And, once again, he swept his stiff right leg up and over Peggy's back, and then pushed his butt into the saddle. But this time he managed to stay on!

Bess, still watching what was happening, smiled.

Now the problem was how to get off. He hadn't thought of that. He slowly edged Peggy away from the fence so he would have some room to dismount, but when he did, he came down hard on his bad leg and ended up in a heap on the ground. The pain in his leg was excruciating, but he dared not make a sound.

Once again the hint of a tear came to his eye, and he considered forgetting the whole thing and spending the rest of the summer in his room, waiting for the day when he would have to go away to boarding school.

"This just ain't gonna work," he whispered.

But once again there was that strange wet feeling of Peggy "kissing" him on the ear, and when he looked up at her, she seemed to be saying, "Come on, Billy. After all I've been through with you, do you expect me to let you give up and go away just because you fell on your leg and hurt your pride?"

So Billy tried again and again, and he practiced getting on and off Peggy all night long. After he got comfortable mounting her from the top rail of the fence, he tried mounting her from the middle rail.

And each time he fell down, he grimaced from the excruciating pain in his right leg while trying not to make a sound.

But then, Peggy would turn to look at him and started pawing the ground, as if to say, "C'mon, I haven't got all night."

Finally, he mounted her while standing on the bottom rail of the fence.

By now, the first light of morning was painting the eastern sky.

Billy was standing on the ground next Peggy. He tried once, twice, three times to mount her from there but he just couldn't get his stiff right leg up over her back.

Bess, who had been watching him all night, once again looked concerned.

Billy tried one more time to mount Peggy from the ground but couldn't.

"I'm sorry, Peggy. I can't do it."

Billy, defeated, walked up and untied Peggy from the fence.

"I gotta get you back in the barn before they wake up."

But when Billy tried to lead Peggy out of the corral, she pulled back and ran to the other side of the corral.

"C'mon, Peggy! This is important!"

When Billy tried to grab her reins, she again ran away from him.

Billy looked worried.

"What's gotten into you, Peggy?

Then Peggy slowly lowered herself to the ground and looked at Billy.

At first Billy didn't understand what she was trying to say, but then he figured it out.

"Why, you old nag!" he said happily. "You want me to get on you, don't you!"

Billy hobbled over to where Peggy was sitting on the ground. Then he stepped over her and settled into the saddle.

"All right, Peg. Let's go."

Peggy stood up so suddenly that Billy almost lost his balance, but he managed to hold on.

Peggy trotted around the corral with Billy in control. He started to scream, "Yahoo!", but then he remembered the sleeping Bess and Diane, so he instead whispered a quiet, "yahoo."

Bess, looking out at what was happening in the corral, smiled and then turned to go back to bed as the curtain fell closed behind her.

After Billy returned Peggy to the barn, he headed over and quietly entered the house, but when he got inside, he realized that Diane was in the kitchen. So, trying not to make any noise, he went into his bedroom.

However, Diane had heard something and walked out of the kitchen. She went to the door to Billy's room and knocked on it.

"Billy, you still asleep? It's time to get up."

When she opened the door and looked in, Billy was in bed with the blankets pulled up to his neck, pretending that he had been there all night.

"You gotta get up," she said.

"I will," answered Billy, turning over. "Just a few more minutes."

Later that day, Bess was working in her garden when Billy walked up.

"Guess what, Granma! I rode Peggy!"

"That's wonderful!" responded Bess. "Where did you ride her to?"

"Well, just in the corral," Billy admitted. "But I'm gonna ride her outside, one of these days!"

"Well, that day will come when it's ready to come," said Bess calmly.

Billy looked over at the corral, a little worried.

"I hope you're right, Grandma."

One day Billy was standing in the corral next to Peggy. The gate to the corral was open.

Billy mounted Peggy and felt quite proud of himself.

But then Wally, Molly and Arthur, all on horseback, rode up. When Billy saw them, his demeanor changed to one of hatred, fear and anger.

"Well, lookee here," said Molly in that annoying squeaky voice of his. "It if tain't the little cripple boy on a big ugly hoss."

Then Arthur spoke:

"My daddy told me you was tryin' to tame 'er for the steeplechase, but we just had to see for ourselves. It hardly seems worth the effort," he said disdainfully.

"I don't need your opinion on anything," Billy snapped back.

"Speaking of needing somethin'...," Arthur said, smirking. "How do you propose to go about getting the money to pay for the entrance fee to the race?"

Billy was shocked — this was the first time he had heard anything about an entrance fee.

"You do know about the entrance fee, don't you?" Arthur continued, snidely.

"Course I do," Billy lied. "It's, uh, what — five dollars, right?

Arthur laughed and Wally and Molly smiled.

"Five dollars? That shows you how much you know! It's fifteen dollars!"

Billy's heart dropped, but he didn't want those no-account boys to know how he felt, so he said, "Don't worry — I'll get it somewhere. Me and Peg will do just fine."

"In that case," asked Wally, "how 'bout racin' us over to the mill and back? Or are ya too skeared?"

"I ain't askeared a nuthin'," Billy answered back. "But Peggy just had a good workout and she's in no shape to do any racin'."

"I thought so," smirked Wally. "You are too skeared."

But then, from out of the barn, came Hector's voice:

"He ain't scared."

Hector appeared from inside the barn.

"He's tellin' the truth."

The three boys turned on their horses to face Hector.

"Now you boys git. You're not welcome her," Hector continued.

"You stay out of this, Mexican!" Molly snarled. "If we wanted your opinion, we'd a asked fer it."

Wally dismounted his horse and said, "Why don't we teach this old Mexican a lesson?"

"You stay away from him, Wally McCoy!" Billy yelled out.

Wally walked toward Hector, who stood his ground.

"Who's gonna stop me?" Wally said out of the side of his mouth. "A little cripple boy like you?"

"Nope," said Billy. "A little cripple boy like me...

Billy quickly rode out of the corral on Peggy and positioned himself between Wally and Hector.

"...and a big ugly hoss!"

For a moment, they all stood there in a standoff. Then Wally looked back up at Arthur for guidance.

Finally, Arthur said, "Come on, boys. These pieces of dirt ain't worth our time."

Wally, relieved, remounted his horse, and the three of them rode off as Hector and Billy watched them go.

"Thank you, Mr. Billy," Hector said. "That was a mighty close call."

"That's all right, Hector," Billy responded. "I ain't ascared a them," he lied.

For a moment, Billy considered taking Peggy for a ride, but in the end he turned Peggy around and rode her back into the corral.

That evening, Billy, Diane and Bess had just finished dinner and Diane was finishing up her after-dinner prayer.

"And thank you for the food which you provided for us. Amen."

"Amen," added Billy.

As Diane stood up and started to clear the table, she added:

"Now I gotta get an early start tomorrow morning, so what's say we all turn in early?"

Billy stood up.

"Uh, Ma. There's somethin' I gotta ask you about."

Diane stopped what she was doing to listen to him.

"What is it, Billy?"

Billy walked up to her.

"Well, you know the steeplechase..."

"What are you talking about?" Diane snapped back. "I told you, I don't want you riding that horse."

"But it only costs fifteen dollars to enter it!" Billy pleaded. "And I was wondering..."

"Fifteen dollars!" said Diane, shaking her head. "Well, I guess that puts an end to that dream! There's no way I can come up with that kind of money."

"But Ma," Billy continued. "If, I mean, when I win the race, we'll get it all back and more!"

"I'm sorry, Billy," Diane answered, "but I don't want to hear about it."

"But...," Billy began, but Diane cut him off.

"No, that's it! Now you get yourself to your room, and I don't want to hear a peep out of you for the rest of the evening!"

Billy, forlorn, dragged himself to his room.

Diane sighed and then went back to clearing the table.

Bess had been seated at the table silently observing the preceding interchange but now decided to speak up.

"What happened to you, Diane? I remember a time when you would have swum across the ocean with one hand tied behind your back if you thought it would help Billy. Where have all your dreams and hopes gone?"

"Where have my dreams gone?" Diane answered, continuing to clear the table. "They were kidnapped by reality, that's where. And as far as my hopes are concerned — what do I have to hope about? My son is a cripple, the man I loved is dead, and the farm he loved is failing. You live in a fantasy world but I have to live in the real world. I'm doing the best I can, and that includes doing all I can to protect Billy from the realities — and the dreams — of the world."

Bess stood up.

"You think you're doing what's best for him, but in 'reality,' to use your term, you're just acting out of fear. Your fear of letting him try to jump a little higher caused Billy's accident, and now it's going to define his life.

"And how can he believe in himself if you don't believe in him yourself?"

"I just don't want him to get hurt," said Diane, stopping what she was doing to think about what Bess had said. "Maybe I'm just afraid he'll lose the race and lose the only hope he has."

Bess spoke: "But if you don't support him, he'll never even get a chance to try."

Bess walked over and tenderly put her hand on Diane's shoulder.

"Remember when you first fell in love with Jed?"

Diane pictured it in her mind. "Yes — it was when he won the steeplechase in '21."

"That wasn't when you fell in love with him," said Bess. "I was watching you that day. You didn't fall in love with him when he finished the race. You fell in love with him when he started it."

Diane thought about what Bess had said.

Then Bess said, "Good night, Didi."

"Good night, Bess," Diane replied.

Bess started to leave, but then Diane called to her: "Bess..."

Bess stopped and turned back towards Diane.

"Yes?"

"Thanks," said Diane.

Bess smiled and left.

Later that night, Diane was in her bed clothes, sitting on the edge of her bed and holding a photograph of Jed that had been taken the day Jed won the steeplechase.

Diane spoke to the photo:

"I don't know what to do, Jed. My life hasn't turned out the way I thought it would. I'm trying to save our family, but instead I'm destroying it. I don't want to marry Mr. Bartlett, but it's the only way I can figure to get out of this mess."

She stood up, walked over to a dresser and placed the photo of Jed on top of it. Then she moved the dresser a few feet to the side.

She knelt down and pulled up a square piece of floor board from where the dresser had been, revealing a pit beneath it. In the pit was a tin can. She picked up the tin can and then went back to sit on the edge of the bed. She pulled some rolled-up money out of the can and counted it out:

"Ten, fifteen, twenty, twenty-one, twenty-two, twenty-three."

She sat there with the money in her hand, thinking...

The next morning when Diane entered the dining room, Billy was seated at the table eating breakfast.

"Billy, I gotta go into town."

She sat down at the table.

"Son, I did some thinkin' last night."

Billy waited expectantly for what she had to say.

"I'm probably making another mistake, but I guess at this point one more mistake don't make no difference." She took his left hand in her right hand and looked into his eyes. "Billy, I love you and I believe in you. And I'm gonna pay your entrance fee for the steeplechase."

Billy was overjoyed to hear this and stood up to hug her.

"Thank you, Ma! Thank you! Thank you!"

Diane tried to pull away from him.

"But you gotta promise me that you'll be careful. And don't go getting your hopes up. A lot of good riders will be in that race."

"Don't worry, Ma!" Billy responded, all excited. "We can do it. I know we can!"

"I must be crazy," said Diane, looking down and then at Billy. "But when you say it like that, I almost believe it myself."

Then Hector whistled from the front yard that he was ready with the carriage.

Diane started to leave.

"Mr. Bartlett's not gonna like it when he hears that I paid for it with money he gave me, but he'll have to live with it.

"Bye, Billy."

When Diane went out, Billy ran to the front door.

Hector helped Diane to get into the carriage as Billy watched.

"Bye, Ma! And you'll see — me and Peg will make you proud!"

Diane snapped the reins and started off in the carriage.

Billy came back in the house.

A little worried, Billy thought about what he had to do.

"Now, all I gotta do is learn to ride her, and all she has to do is learn to jump."

Later that day, Billy and Bess were seated on the swingchair on the front porch of her shed. Bess was peeling some pea pods and dropping the peas into a basket on her lap.

"I don't know what to do, Grandma. I'm still too scared to ride her."

Bess stopped her work and turned and said to Billy, tenderly:

"Billy, there will be all sorts of barriers blocking your way in life. Fear is just another barrier. You can take the long way and try and go around it, but the quickest way is to just barge through it. Either that or jump right over it."

Bess got up.

"Least that's what Aries, the Greek God of war, was telling me t'other day."

All of a sudden, she started to totter, and then she fainted to the ground.

Billy jumped up and went over to her.

"Grandma?" he pleaded frantically. "Are you OK?"

But she didn't respond.

In a panic, Billy hobbled as fast as he could towards the barn.

"Hector!" he yelled.

Hector appeared from inside the barn. He had a wrench in his hand and grease on his clothes.

"What's the matter, son?" he asked.

Billy hobbled over to him.

"It's Grandma Bess! She's sick! We gotta tell the doctor!"

But Billy and Hector both knew that Diane had taken the rig to town.

Billy looked around frantically, trying to figure out a solution. Then his eyes fell on Peggy, who was standing in the corral looking at him.

"Hector! Get the saddle!"

When they had finished getting Peggy saddled up, Hector helped Billy to mount her.

"Here you go."

Billy turned Peggy around.

"Good luck, son," said Hector.

"Take care of Grandma," Billy responded.

Billy sat there for a moment to gather his courage. Then:

"OK, girl. Let's go."

He gently dug his heels into Peggy and she took off in a gentle, but wobbly, trot.

Peggy, with Billy holding on for his life, wobbled down the road. She was moving as though she was old, broken down, scared and completely out of shape.

"What's wrong, girl?" Billy wondered. "Don't you know how to run?"

When they arrived at Doc Wilson's home/office, Billy yelled, "Whoa," but Peggy stopped so suddenly that Billy was thrown forward and only avoided being thrown off by grabbing her neck.

Billy quickly dismounted and ran inside.

"Doc! Doc! It's my Grandma!"

Later that afternoon when Billy and Peggy, both exhausted, arrived back at the Diangelo spread, Doc Wilson's car was parked in front of Bess's shed.

Billy was greeted by Hector, who helped him to dismount.

"You made it!"

"Yeah," said Billy, "but I just forgot to teach her one thing."

"What's that?" asked Hector.

"The meaning of the word 'whoa'!"

Doc Wilson, a grandfatherly-looking man in his early sixties, came out the front door of Bess's shed, and Billy ran over to him.

"How is she, Doc? She gonna be OK?"

"She's all right, son," the doctor said. "She just needs some rest."

"Can I see her?" asked Billy?

"Sure," said the doctor. "Just don't get her too excited."

When Billy entered his grandmother's shed, she was lying in bed. She didn't look good...

"Grandma?" Billy whispered.

... but she perked up a bit when Billy entered the room.

Bess looked over at him. "Hi, Billy. Hector told me that you rode Peggy. I'm so proud of you."

Billy sat on the edge of the bed.

"I'm just glad we made it in time," Billy said.

Then Billy took her hands in his.

"I'm so sorry you're sick, Grandma."

"Don't worry about me, Billy," answered Bess. "You just take care of yourself."

Then, Bess, exhausted, closed her eyes and was soon fast asleep.

The next time Mr. Bartlett came to visit, Billy's mother told Mr. Bartlett that Billy planned to enter the steeplechase race. Mr. Bartlett was outraged, not because he was afraid that Billy would defeat his son, but because he was afraid that Billy might get hurt again and that he would be stuck paying his medical costs.

"It's a crazy idea, Didi. And don't you think I'll pay if he gets injured before we get married. That's something you two will just have to work out between yourselves."

Diane was hurt by Mr. Bartlett's selfishness.

"Why, Mr. Bartlett, I am shocked to hear you say that. Don't forget that once we are married, I will expect you to treat Billy like your own son."

Then Mr. Bartlett said something that he immediately regretted.

"Well, my own son has more sense than to risk getting thrown off a horse after it already happened once before."

Billy's mother exploded. "That does it! Either you apologize or I want you out of my house until you do!"

"There's no reason to apologize for common sense, Didi," Mr. Bartlett shot back as he stood up. "I will leave, and I'm not coming back until you talk some sense into that boy of yours."

And with that, Mr. Bartlett walked out the door, got into his car, and disappeared down the road. And as soon as he was out of sight, Billy's mother ran into her bedroom and fell onto her bed.

For a moment, Billy, who had been listening to the whole conversation from his room, was filled with doubt. He wondered if he was making a mistake by challenging Arthur Bartlett in the steeplechase. Maybe it would be best if he just accepted the fact that he would be going away to boarding school and let his mother get married and have a happy life with Mr. Bartlett.

But then he realized that he wasn't going to compete in the steeplechase only for himself and his mother — he was also going to use some of the prize money to rescue Peggy.

So that decided it. He would race and, as his grandmother would say, let the gods decide the outcome.

A few days later, Carol was sitting on Bess's front steps watching Billy ride Peggy.

Billy and Hector had put some low piles of lumber, hay, oil drums, and so on, in an open space near the corral. Billy was practicing jumping over them on Peggy as Hector stood by to coach and give advice, but the obstacles were so low that Peggy was really stepping over them rather than jumping.

Bess, looking quite frail, came out of the front door of her shed holding a glass of lemonade.

"Here you are, dear," she said as she handed the glass to Carol.

"Thank you, Miss Diangelo," said Carol before taking a sip.

Then Carol and Bess turned their attention to the show Billy and Peggy were putting on.

"Why don't they use higher hurdles?" wondered Carol.

"Maybe they are both too scared," Bess suggested.

"If only they could win the race..."

"Oh, I wouldn't worry about that," said Bess.

Carol turned to face Bess.

"Do you think they have a chance?"

Bess looked out at Billy with a knowing smile on her face.

"Something tells me that they do."

Later that afternoon after Carol left to go home, Billy was approaching the front of his house when a telephone installer exited carrying a tool chest, followed by Diane.

"It's all set, Ma'am," the man said to Diane. "It's a party line, but it works like a charm. "

"Thanks," Diane said. "We thought, with my mother-in-law's health problems and all..."

"Just remember," the man interrupted her. "Yours is two short rings."

The telephone installer left and Billy and Diane entered the house.

"Isn't it wonderful, Billy! Now we can call anyone and they can call us! And it was all paid for by Mr. Bartlett. Now you see, he isn't such a bad person."

"If that's what you think is important," murmured Billy.

Just then, the phone rang — two short rings.

"O'm'gosh, Billy! That's our ring. A call already!" Diane said, excited.

Diane answered the phone.

"Hello? Oh, hello, Phil."

Billy made a face.

"Yes, it's wonderful. Thank you so much. It was very thoughtful of you.

"Yes.

"Yes.

She paused to listen to what he was saying. Then:

"Yes, that would be wonderful. I'll see you there. Bye."

She hung up the phone and then spoke to Billy.

"Mr. Bartlett invited me to the dance at the town hall Friday night. That must mean he's ready to announce our engagement publicly."

Billy lowered his head down, walked into his room, lay down on the bed and buried his head in the pillow.

The next day, Billy and Carol were on their scooters, pushing along slowly next to each other.

"If only she didn't marry Mr. Bartlett!" Billy thought out loud.

"Maybe she could marry someone else," Carol mentioned casually.

Hearing this, Billy stopped in his tracks, surprising Carol, who stopped too.

Billy was thinking...

"Is something wrong?" Carol asked him.

"Nope," replied Billy. "'fact, something might have just turned out right. C'mon!"

With that, Billy turned his scooter around and headed back quickly in the direction they just came from.

"Hey — wait for me!" Carol called out after him.

Carol pushed along on her scooter trying to catch up to him.

A few minutes later, Carol and Billy pulled up in front of Axton Twilly's store on their scooters and lay the scooters down.

"So you unnnerstand what you gotta do?" Billy whispered conspiratorially.

"Yes," replied Carol.

Carol entered the store while Billy waited outside.

Inside the store, Axton was dusting a display.

"Hello, Mr. Twilly!" Carol called out brightly.

Axton, happily surprised, looked up.

"Why, hello there, Carol. What can I do for you?"

"Well, I was thinkin' a buying a birthday gift for my auntie," Carol said, putting her hand to her chin and pretending to actually think. "She's about your wife's age…"

Axton blushed.

"Why, I don't know where you hear'd that, Carol. I'm not married."

Carol was happy to hear this response.

"You're not?" she smiled.

"No," said Axton shyly. "I never been married. Just never got around to it, I guess."

"OK. Thanks!" said Carol happily as she turned to leave.

"But what about your aunt's birthday gift?" asked Axton, puzzled.

"That's OK," said Carol as she was leaving. "It's not for another month anyway."

Axton stood there confused for a moment and then went back to his work.

When Carol got out on the walkway in front of Axton's store, she gave a "thumbs-up" sign to Billy.

Billy then entered the store.

Axton looked up and was happy to see him, as well.

"Why, hello there, Billy. Say, your little friend Carol was just in here...

"Do you like to dance, Mr. Twilly?" Billy interrupted him.

"Whah?" said Axton, taken aback.

"My ma told me that there's a dance at the town hall Friday night..."

"Oh, I'm not much of a dancer," said Axton.

"...and she said she was hoping you'd be there," Billy continued.

Axton was happily surprised to hear this.

"Really?"

"Yes," said Billy. "'fact, she said she hoped she could have a dance with you!"

Axton once again blushed.

"I thought your ma was being courted by Mr. Bartlett."

"Oh, he's sweet on her," Billy said, "but she don't return it."

"Well, in that case," said Axton, thinking, "I guess it would be a shame to disappoint her!"

"Great!" said Billy. "I'll tell her you'll be there."

Billy turned to leave.

"Is that all you came in for?" Axton asked, once again puzzled.

"Oh, I was gonna buy something," said Billy on his way out, "but I forgot what it was."

Axton shook his head and smiled and then went back to what he was doing.

Then he stopped for a moment, thought about something, smiled again, and then returned to what he was doing.

When Billy exited the store, he gave a "thumbs-up" to Carol.

Then they hopped on their scooters and started off down the main street.

"But what are we gonna do about Mr. Bartlett?" Carol worried.

"We'll think of somethin'," said Billy, confidently. "Or maybe one of my Grandma's gods will help out!" he joked.

Carol smiled at the idea.

That Friday night, the town hall was all lit up. From inside could be heard the sound of music and of people enjoying themselves. More people were streaming into the hall.

Billy and Diane came walking towards the town hall.

"Billy, where in tarnation did you ever get interested in going to a dance?"

"I jus' wanna see what it's all about," Billy lied again. "That's all."

When Diane stopped and looked at her watch, Billy practically started to drag her towards the front door of the town hall.

"C'mon, Ma — we're gonna be late!"

"I don't know what your hurry is," Diane said. "I'm not supposed to meet Mr. Bartlett for fifteen more minutes, and he's usually late, anyway."

The hall was festooned with cheap decorations (streamers, posters, balloons, etc.), but the band was playing lively music and everyone seemed be having a good time, visiting or sipping the punch or dancing.

While Diane stared at the proceedings blankly, Billy scanned the room trying to locate the two people he was looking for.

When he spotted both of them, he and Carol made eye contact, and Carol came over to where Diane and Billy were standing.

"Hello, Mrs. Diangelo! Enjoying the dance?"

"Oh, hello, Carol. Yes, it's nice to be out again. I haven't been anywhere since my Jed died."

While Carol occupied Diane's attention, Billy slipped away.

Billy walked up to Axton.

"Hello, Mr. Twilly!"

"Oh, hello, Billy."

"Say, my Ma is standing over there..."

He pointed to where his mother and Carol were standing.

"...and she was just hopin' you'd come over 'n' ask her for a dance."

Axton, ever the shy one, said, "Well, all right, Billy, if you say so."

So Billy led the way as he and Axton made their way over where Carol and Diane were standing.

"Uh, hello, Mrs. Diangelo," Axton said nervously. "I was just wondering if you would do me the honor..."

"Oh, I don't know...,"said Diane, looking around for advice from anyone who could give it.

But then Billy, who was now standing behind her, literally pushed her forward into Axton's arms.

"Oh!" said Diane, surprised.

"Thank you!" said Axton, happy.

Axton and Diane then walked towards the center of the hall and started to dance.

Billy and Carol stood side by side watching, proud of what they had accomplished.

Then Billy, still looking straight ahead, allowed his hand to wander over and take Carol's hand in his.

Surprised, she glanced at him for a moment and then once again turned her gaze forward, only now she had an even bigger smile on her face.

When the song ended, Diane stepped back from Axton. They were soon joined by Carol and Billy.

"Thank you, Axton. I enjoyed that," said Diane, smiling.

The music started up again.

Diane looked at the door.

"But I'd better sit this one out..."

"If you say so," said Axton, disappointed.

But Billy and Carol quickly interceded: Billy stood behind Diane and Carol stood behind Axton, and they pushed Diane and Axton as they talked:

"Come on, Ma!" Billy said. "It's just one more dance.

"C'mon, Axton!" said Carol.

By now Axton and Diane were back in each other's arms.

When Diane said, "Well, I guess one more couldn't hurt," a big smile spread across Axton's face. He took her hands in his and they start dancing again.

Carol and Billy looked at each other and shared a glance of triumph.

Later, when the band had taken a short break and Axton had gone to get Diane a drink, Diane looked at her watch.

"I can't understand why Mr. Bartlett isn't here yet. He's never this late."

Axton showed up with a drink for Diane.

She and Axton became engaged in conversation so they didn't hear what Billy and Carol said next.

"Did you do something to his car?" Billy asked Carol in a whisper.

"No," replied Carol, puzzled. "I thought you were gonna."

Billy shook his head. Both he and Carol were mystified as to what had delayed Mr. Bartlett.

Meanwhile, out on a country road, Mr. Bartlett was changing a flat tire on his car just as the sun was setting. His sleeves were rolled up and his shirt was greasy.

When he twisted the tool to loosen the lug nuts on the tire, it slipped and hit him in the right foot. He jumped up, danced on his left foot, and howled.

At that very moment, Bess was seated, knitting, on the rocking bench. She looked off in the distance, smiled, and then went back to her knitting.

Later that night, there were fewer people in the Town Hall since many had already left. The band was playing a slow song.

Axton and Diane were dancing, holding each other close. And Billy and Carol were, too.

When the band finished the song, the band leader stood up and said, "Well, thank you all for coming. And see ya next month!"

The band members started to pack up their things as the attendees said their good-byes and started to leave.

Axton and Diane faced each other. He was holding her hand.

"Thank you, Axton," said Diane, breathless and in love. "I had a wonderful time."

"You know I never would have come tonight if Billy hadn't told me what you said," said Axton.

"What?" said Diane, confused.

But at just that moment, Mr. Bartlett, with grease all over his face and shirt, suddenly appeared at the door of the hall. He was mad, and he became even madder when he saw Axton and Diane talking to each other and holding hands.

Because he had hurt his foot when he was changing the tire, he limped slightly as he stormed over to Diane and Axton.

"Just what do you think you're doing?" he angrily demanded.

Diane was mortified and Axton didn't know what to think.

Carol and Billy could only look on in horror.

Mr. Bartlett tore Diane's hand away from Axton's and then said right in her face:

"This is some way for a widow woman to act!"

Then he turned to Axton:

"And you — you have some nerve courting a woman who is betrothed to another man!"

Axton found it hard to find the words.

"But Mr. Bartlett, I had no idea!"

Mr. Bartlett continued:

"If you ever so much as look at her again, I'll make sure you never work or own a piece of property in this county again!"

Then Mr. Bartlett started to pull Diane towards the door.

"C'mon, Didi!"

Mr. Bartlett pulled Diane, who was now close to tears, all the way out of the hall and then stopped to talk to her.

"And you! If you don't start getting some sense into you, the wedding is off!

Diane could barely speak.

"Please, just leave me. Just leave."

Mr. Bartlett gave her one more dirty look before storming off.

Billy came out of the hall and approached Diane. Carol soon appeared in the doorway of the hall and watched what is going on.

"I'm sorry, Ma. I didn't know..."

Axton appeared at the door of the hall, standing behind Carol. He called over to Diane:

"You OK, Diane?"

Diane looked up at him.

"I'm sorry, Axton," she said sadly. "I'm sorry."

Then, to Billy:

"C'mon, Billy. Let's go home."

They walked off, holding on to each other, leaving Carol and Axton standing in the door of the hall.

A few days later, Billy rode up to his house on his scooter. He sensed something was wrong when Hector came out of their house (he usually never went in there) with a worried expression on his face.

Billy jumped off his scooter and hobbled over to Hector.

"Hector! What's wrong?"

"Your granma's been taken ill, son. Your ma took her over to Doc Wilson's. He just called. She's gonna hafta stay there a while."

Billy absorbed this news for a moment and then headed for the barn.

When Billy arrived at Doc Wilson's place riding Peggy, the Diangelo carriage was already parked out front.

He quickly dismounted and went in.

Billy was shown into the room by Doc Wilson. Bess was in a bed, and Diane was standing next to her.

"Here she is, son. Don't be too long."

Then Doc Wilson motioned to Diane and said, "Diane — can I speak to you a moment?", and then left.

Diane exchanged a glance with Billy and put her hand on his shoulder and then followed Doc Wilson out of the room.

Billy approached the bed, where Bess was resting comfortably with her eyes closed. She looked very old and gray.

"Gran'ma?"

Bess opened her eyes and a smile came to her face when she realized that Billy was there. She spoke with some difficulty.

"Why, hello there, Billy. I been expectin' you."

"Gran'ma, what happened?"

"Oh, just a little dizzy spell, is all. I wanted to go back to bed but Diane insisted on bringing me over here. And now Doc won't let me go back home."

Billy sat down on the corner of the bed.

"Are you gonna be all right?"

"Well, to tell you the truth, I don't think I have much more time left on this earth, Billy. In fact, last night while I was asleep, Morpheus came to me and told me I was going to be called to heaven soon."

Tears started to form in Billy's eyes as he took Bess's hand.

"But that's all right. I'm ready to go whenever it's my time. I just hope it's not a bumpy ride."

Billy stood up and moved over so he was standing closer to Bess's face.

"Gran'ma, please don't talk like that. Why, you cain't go yet. Not until I win the steeplechase race!"

Bess managed a smile.

"All right, Billy. I promise I won't go until after the race."

"Thanks, Gran'ma. You'll see — me and Peg will make you proud!"

Bess reached over with her free hand and took Billy's hand in both of her hands.

"Just remember that whatever happens, I will always believe in you," she said, looking up into his eyes. "The important thing is that you believe in yourself. And don't worry if you don't win the race. The important thing is to try, to compete. Remember: quitin' is losin'. Even if you finish last, that's a victory all by itself. And whatever you do for the rest of your life, I'll always be rooting for you, either from down here or from up there."

By now Bess was too tired to continue, so she released her grip on his hands, let her head fall back into the pillow and closed her eyes.

Billy wiped a tear from his cheek and whispered, "I'll remember, Gran'ma. I'll remember."

One day soon thereafter, Billy was seated on Peggy and Hector was standing on the ground nearby with a watch in his hand. Near them was a hurdle that was higher than the hurdles they had been practicing on earlier.

"Remember," said Hector. "This hurdle is the same height as the hurdles in the race. So you got to make it over. OK?

Billy nodded seriously.

"OK."

"Ready?" asked Hector.

Billy nodded that he was ready.

While looking at the face of the watch in his left hand, Hector signaled with his right hand and said, "Go!"

Billy dug his heals into Peggy's sides and she took off.

Peggy and Billy were moving better across the countryside than when Billy had gone to get medical help for his grandmother, but they were still not moving smoothly.

They came to a hedge row. Peggy slowed down and then jumped and barely managed to make it over.

In the distance, the steeple of a church appeared. As they rode towards it, the steeple got larger and then the church came into view.

Billy and Peggy moved around the church and then headed back towards the farm, where Hector was nervously waiting for them, alternately looking at the horizon and looking down at the watch in his hand.

Finally, Peggy and Billy appeared over the far hillside and came down towards the hurdle near where Hector is standing.

"C'mon — you can do it," Hector said under his breath.

Peggy was gaining speed as she approached the hurdle.

But at the last minute, Billy pulled on the reins causing Peggy to veer around the hurdle.

Hector was disappointed, and Billy was heart-broken and ashamed.

As Billy dismounted, he said, "I just couldn't do it, Hector. I'm sorry."

Hector took Peggy's reins from Billy and said, somberly:

"Yo tambien, muchacho. Lo siento, mucho."

Hector led Peggy away, leaving Billy standing there alone to deal with what just happened.

At that very moment in the Bartlett home, Mr. Bartlett violently slapped Arthur in the face, sending him back on his heels and onto a sofa.

"Don't you ever talk to me like that again!" Mr. Bartlett said, breathing fire. "Do you understand?"

Arthur, almost in tears, felt his sore jaw where his father had just slapped him.

"What do you want me to do, Pa?" Arthur whined.

"I want you to win the race!" his father answered firmly.

"So, what's the problem?" asked Arthur. "You don't think that run-down horse can win, do you? I've been watching her. She can't even jump."

Mr. Bartlett walked over to Arthur and waved his finger in Arthur's face.

"That's not the point. I don't even want them to compete. If that boy gets hurt again, I'll end up paying for it. Do you understand?"

"Yes, Pa," Arthur answered.

Calming down a little bit, Mr. Bartlett walked away from Arthur.

"Do whatever you have to. Just don't tell me what it is."

Arthur, regaining some of his strength, stood up.

"OK, Pa. I'll take care of it."

After Arthur left, Mr. Bartlett said (to no one in particular):

"I don't know why, but something about that horse worries me..."

That night, Diane arrived in the carriage, driven by Hector, at Doc Wilson's place. She was very worried.

Diane and Doc Wilson walked to the open door of the room in which Bess was resting in bed and looked in.

"She may not have much time left. I thought you'd want to know."

"Thanks," Diane said and then entered Bess's room.

She knelt down next to the bed where Bess was and reached out and took Bess's hand.

"Bess, it's me — Diane," she said softly.

Bess opened her eyes and looked around. Then she recognized Diane.

"Oh, hello, dear," she said in a weak voice that was barely audible. "I been expectin' you."

Diane could barely hold back her tears.

"How are you, dear?"

"Not bad. Not bad at all."

Diane found it hard to find the right words.

"Bess, I just wanted to see you... to tell you how sorry I am about the way I messed everything up."

Bess made a face as if she couldn't understand what Diane meant, so Diane continued.

"I mean, Billy, Jed, the farm — I feel responsible for it all."

Bess half sat up.

"Oh, no, dear — you got it all wrong."

Diane was puzzled by her response.

Then Bess got a contented look on her face.

"Why, everything's going just like it's supposed to. You'll see..."

Bess fell back on the pillow...

"You'll see... It's goin' jus' like it's s'posed ta go. Jus' like it's supposed to..."

...and she was soon fast asleep.

Diane stood up and then leaned over and tenderly kissed Bess on the forehead.

Billy was waiting anxiously for Diane's return. When Diane walked in the door, Billy rushed over to meet her.

"How is she, Ma? She gonna make it?"

"I don't know, Billy," Diane answered. "It don't look good.

Diane started to hang up her coat when Billy spoke to her again.

"Ma..."

"Yes, Billy," she said as she turned towards him.

"I know I promised Bess, but...I don't think I can do it."

"Do what?"

"Race. The only time I tried to jump a hurdle on Peggy, I chickened out. It's just no use."

Diane knelt down in front of Billy and put her hands on his shoulders.

"Listen, Billy, nobody — not even the gods — can tell if you're gonna win that race. But one thing I've learned from Bess is that it's important that you at least try."

Billy looked down, but Diane lifted his chin with her finger so he was looking at her again.

"Right?"

Billy smiled.

"Right!"

Diane pulled Billy to her and hugged him. Then she released her hug.

"Now get to bed. We got an exciting day tomorrow!"

"OK, Ma," he answered.

Billy started to walk towards his bedroom, but then he stopped and turned back towards Diane.

"Ma..."

"Yes, Billy."

"I'm sorry I blamed you for my accident. I shoulda obeyed Pa when he told me not to try jumping with Betty."

Diane smiled.

"That's all right, Billy. We've all said and done some things we regret. Let's both say an extra prayer for Bess before we go to bed, OK?

"And while we're at it, why don't we say a little prayer for us, too?"

Now Billy smiled.

"OK, Ma. And Ma...," he said with moist eyes.

"Yes, Billy?"

"I love you."

Diane replied with moist eyes as well:

"I love you, too, Billy."

Billy turned and entered his bedroom.

Billy got up at dawn and, trying to be as quiet as possible, carefully exited his room and crossed the living room to the front door.

He let himself out the front door, making sure not to let the screen door slam

Then he walked around the side of the house to where Hector was standing with Peggy, already saddled up.

"Thanks, Hector," said Billy.

"You go win that race, son," Hector said.

But just then two hooded riders came tearing into the farm, whooping and hollering.

Billy and Hector stepped back when they saw the two ghost-like riders.

A light went on in Diane's bedroom window.

The two riders, hollering like banshees, rode over to Peggy, knocking Hector down.

One of them slapped Peggy on the rump, scaring her so that she pulled away from Billy's grip and ran off, followed closely by the ghost riders who were still chasing her and yelling at her.

Shocked, Billy watched the three horses disappeared in the distance.

Hector was still lying on the ground, knocked out, when Diane, wearing a bathrobe, appeared.

"What happened?" said Diane, worried.

"They got Peggy, Ma!" Billy screamed frantically. "They got Peggy!"

"You go see if you can find her." Diane leaned down to attend to Hector. "I'll see to Hector."

Billy hurried as fast as he could in the direction where the two riders and Peggy had disappeared.

After a few minutes, Billy reached a meadow near a grove of trees.

The sun had now risen in the sky and Billy was near exhausted from frantically looking for the horse. Then he looked over and saw Peggy in the grove of trees.

"Peg!"

Billy went over to the grove, but when he got near Peggy, she moved away from him, just as she had when he had first tried to approach him.

"O'm'gosh, Peggy, it's OK," he said, pleadingly. "It's me — Billy."

He tried to approach her again, but she just moved away from him again.

"I know what you're thinkin', that it was a mistake to trust us humans, but we're not all like those two boys. I don't know how to convince you, but you jus' gotta believe me. It's important to me and it's important to Bess. And, you know what? It's important to you, too.

"Now, will you trust me?"

Peggy looked at him a moment...

...and then walked over to him.

Billy, tears flowing, hugged her.

"Oh, Peg!"

Back at the farm, Doc Wilson was hunched over Hector attending to him as Carol and Diane looked on.

"He got quite a knock to the head," Doc Wilson said, "but he'll be all right."

Then Carol saw Billy ride up on Peggy.

"You got him!" she screamed.

"How's Hector?" asked Billy.

Doc Wilson answered:

"He'll be all right, son, but..."

He looked at his watch.

"...you'd best be hurryin' if you want to be in that race."

Billy looked at Diane.

"It's OK, Billy. Doc Wilson offered to take us over in his car. We'll see you there."

"OK!" said Billy and then took off on Peggy.

"And may God — or the gods — be with you," Diane said, watching him go.

Billy and Peggy wobbled across the countryside as fast as they could.

At the county fairgrounds, the grandstands were filled with excited people, including Mr. Bartlett, who had a gruff expression on his face. He looked at his watch, worried.

The two judges of the race walked up to him.

"Mornin', Mr. Bartlett," said the first judge, tipping his hat.

"Mornin'," replied Mr. Bartlett, stiffly.

The first race judge cleared his throat and then said:

"Fine day for a race..."

"Look — I brought the prize money, if that's what you want to know," growled Mr. Bartlett.

"I didn't mean to doubt..." the judge began, but Mr. Bartlett cut him off:

"But I'll hold on to it until my son, I mean, until the race is over. Just make sure there isn't any cheatin' or other shenanigans."

"No reason to worry about that, Mr. Bartlett," the second race judge spoke up. "We got Rufus out at the church to make sure all the horses go round it, fair and square."

Then Molly and Wally appeared and entered the stands. They looked for Mr. Bartlett, and when they caught his eye, he raised his eyebrows as if in asking a question. They both nodded and smiled smugly in reply.

Mr. Bartlett let a slight smile form on his lips before he caught himself and once again turned his attention to the race track in front of him, where about twenty horses and riders (including Arthur Bartlett and his horse) were walking towards the starting line.

Diane, Doc Wilson, Carol and Hector showed up. Hector had a bandage on his head, and when he took his place in the stands, some people standing nearby moved away from him.

Diane walked over and stood stiffly next to Mr. Bartlett, who looked at his watch.

"You're late," he said without even looking at her.

Diane scanned the crowd, looking for Axton. She saw him about ten rows up, but when he turned his head to look down at her, she quickly averted her gaze and looked down at the track.

Just then, at the entrance to the race track behind the starting line, Billy rode Peggy onto the track.

In front of them, all the other racers were already lined up, with Arthur Bartlett next to the rail.

When the starter raised his pistol, Peggy and Billy were still ten yards behind the starting line.

The starter pulled the trigger: BANG!

And the horses were off!

The crowd stood up and cheered them on.

Arthur Bartlett quickly took the lead.

But Billy and Peggy had not yet even moved.

"Well, Peg, this is it," said Billy, determined.

Now the attention of the spectators was divided between the group of racers who were disappearing in the distance on their right and the lone late-arriving rider on their left who had not yet even started the race.

Peggy held her head up, ready to go.

Diane smiled when she realized that it was Billy and Peggy.

Mr. Bartlett turned to see what Diane was reacting to, and a look of surprise came over his face when he too realized that Billy and Peggy had made it to the race.

He glared at Molly and Wally, who shrugged their shoulders as if to say, "We don't know what happened."

Billy and Peggy were now at the starting line.

"Let's just give it a try. OK, Peg?" said Billy.

He dug his heels into Peggy's sides and held on as Peggy wobbled down the track in front of the crowd and then disappeared in the same direction that the other riders had disappeared.

All but one of the pack of horses made it over the first hedge on their first try. The pack headed off for the next hurdle.

Billy and Peggy appeared, but then stopped.

Billy whispered in Peggy's ear.

"The first jump is nice and low, so let's just make it over and then we can go home, OK?" he said.

Peggy managed to get up some speed as she approached the first jump.

But she turned away at the last moment.

Billy rode her a short way back and then turned her around.

"C'mon, Peg. I know you're tired out, but you can do it."

Once again, Billy dug his heels into Peggy's sides and she got up some speed as she approached the first jump.

But once again she turned away at the last moment.

But Billy was not willing to give up yet.

"I believe in you, Peg, even if no one else does."

Then, without Billy even prodding her, Peggy took off heading for the first jump. She was going faster and faster, to the extent that Billy had to hold on tight.

She approached the hurdle, jumped, and… and..

A large majestic wing magically appeared on each side of her body, and...

She literally flew over the hurdle!

In her room where she was lying at Doc Wilson's place, a slight smile came to Bess's face.

Billy was shocked and could hardly talk.

"What chou doin', Peg? Don't you know you're s'posed to come down again?"

Billy held on for dear life as Peggy continued to fly across the countryside towards the other horses and the church steeple in the distance.

Rufus was at the church to make sure that all the horses did indeed make it around. He was seated leaning back in a chair and drinking whiskey right out of a bottle, so he was well on his way to being drunk.

When the other racers tore around the church and steeple, Rufus nodded at them and smiled an "I-don't-feel-no-pain" smile.

But when soon thereafter Billy and Peggy flew around the steeple, Rufus was so shocked that he fell over backward. Then he looked suspiciously at the bottle of whiskey in his hand and then threw it away.

Across the countryside, Peggy just kept on flying over one hurdle after another.

When she had almost caught up with the other riders, she landed behind them and her wings disappeared.

Now Peggy was jumping over the hurdles like a normal horse and, one by one, she was passing the other riders.

There was just one more rider in front of them — Arthur Bartlett — and he was tearing along.

There were now no more hurdles, and Arthur was slapping his horse in the rump. In fact, he was going so fast that Peggy had trouble overtaking him.

Arthur looked back and when he saw Billy and Peggy right behind him, he was so surprised that he lost his concentration for a moment and his horse fell out of its gait.

Now, Peggy was running neck and neck with Arthur's horse! Arthur leaned over and tried to whip Peggy in the head, but this just made her run faster.

In the stands, the people were craning their necks, waiting expectantly for the return of the horses. And then they saw one...

It was Billy and Peggy, followed by Arthur and then the other horses!

Diane, Hector, Axton, Carol, Mr. Bartlett, Wally and Molly couldn't believe their eyes!

On the track, Arthur did his best to chase Billy and Peggy but Billy and Peggy passed the finish line first!

At Doc Wilson's place, a big wide smile came to Bess's face, as if she had just seen Billy win the race from her bed.

Carol ran down to the track to get near Billy and Peggy.

On the track, a photographer ran over and took a picture of Billy seated atop Peggy.

The other riders were animatedly gesturing and discussing what just happened.

In the stands, the crowd was in an uproar. Mr. Bartlett was arguing with the two race judges. The first judge was holding the prize trophy while the second judge was pointing to some lines in the official race rules.

Billy dismounted where Carol was waiting for him, and they gave each other a hug.

"I don't know how Peg did it, but I got a hunch my grandma had something to do with it!" Billy exulted.

By now Arthur had arrived at where his father was standing in the stands.

"I swear to God, Pa, the only way he could have won is if he cheated," he protested.

"I agree," said his father.

Mr. Bartlett jabbed his finger into the chest of the first race judge.

"I say he cheated, and I'm not giving him the money!"

By now, Rufus had shown up.

The first race judge spoke to Mr. Bartlett:

"Now Rufus, here, was at the church. Let's ask him if that horse went around the steeple."

"Are you kidding?" replied Mr. Bartlett. "He's so drunk, he couldn't tell a horse from a goat."

But the first race judge turned and asked him, "You haven't been drinking, have you, Rufus?"

All eyes turn to Rufus.

"Not anymore!" he said, wide-eyed.

"So — did he?" the second race judge asked him.

Rufus looked confused.

Speaking slowly and clearly, the first race judge then asked him again:

"Did the horse that Billy Diangelo was riding make it around the steeple?"

Rufus thought for a moment and then slowly responded.

"Yes, he did indeed make it around..."

"There — ya see?" the second judge said, smiling.

"...only..."

"Only what?" demanded Mr. Bartlett. "Out with it, man!"

"Only... he was flyin'!"

Mr. Bartlett shook his head in disgust...

"Oh, my God!"

...and started to walk away, but Rufus followed after him.

"No, it's true, Mr. Bartlett. He had wings and ever'thin'!"

"Go home and dry out!" Mr. Bartlett snarled.

Mr. Bartlett pushed Rufus back and started to walk away, but Axton blocked his path.

"Not so fast."

"What do you want?" said Mr. Bartlett angrily.

"I just want the boy to get what's comin' to him," replied Axton.

Mr. Bartlett started to push by Axton...

"Get out of my way."

...but Axton grabbed Mr. Bartlett's shoulder and spun him around.

"I'm sorry to have to do this, Mr. Bartlett..."

He hauled off and decked him.

"...but you had it comin'."

Arthur, in shock, wordlessly watched what had happened to his father, but the people standing in the vicinity all cheered

Mr. Bartlett, lying on the floor of the stands, rubbed his chin with a stunned expression on his face.

Axton reached down to where Mr. Bartlett was lying and reached into a pocket inside Mr.

Bartlett's coat. He pulled out the envelope that had the prize money in it.

Axton walked over and took the trophy from the hands of the second race judge. Then he walked over and handed the trophy and the envelope of prize money to Diane, who then hugged him.

Beside the track, Hector and Doc Wilson were talking to a policeman and pointing to Molly and Wally, who took off running down the track.

Billy got back up on Peggy, and they took off in pursuit of Wally and Molly, as did the policeman.

Billy and Peggy quickly overtook the fleeing Molly and Wally and stopped in front of them.

Molly and Wally had to stop, and the policeman grabbed them.

In the stands, as Mr. Bartlett stormed off, he yelled to everyone and no one in particular, "You'll pay for this! You all will!"

But Axton and Diane were too busy kissing to pay any attention to him.

Billy rode back to where Carol was.

"I gotta go see how my grandma is doing. You come over with Doc Wilson."

Carol nodded her assent.

Billy and Peggy shot down the race track and out the gate they had come in earlier.

When they approached Doc Wilson's place, the strange golden cloud was hovering in the sky.

Peggy, with Billy on her, raced up and stopped in front of Doc Wilson's home/office.

Billy dismounted.

"You stay here, Peg. I'll be right back."

Once inside, he went directly to the room where Bess was. Her eyes were closed and she looked terrible.

"Gran'ma, it's me, Billy," he cried. "We won the race, Gran'ma, we won! And you're never gonna believe it, but Peggy can fly!

Bess opened her eyes with some difficulty and spoke to Billy in a barely audible voice.

"I know, Billy! I been expecting you. And now I want to explain about Peggy."

She took a deep breath, gathered her strength and sat halfway up.

"You see, 'Peggy' is not her real name. Her real name is 'Pegasus.' Zeus knew my time here on earth was almost over, so he lent her to me so I could ride her up to heaven. But when she arrived, I realized she was too wild for me to ride. But she wasn't used to getting around without her wings, either."

Billy listened intently.

"She needed someone to teach how to be an earthly horse. That's why I asked you to see if you could tame her."

Bess managed to push herself up onto her elbows.

"Now it's time for me to go, Billy. Actually, I was ready some weeks ago, but Zeus let me wait until after the race."

With Billy's help, Bess pushed herself up into a seated position on the side of the bed.

"Do you think you could help me?" she asked.

"Sure," said Billy seriously. "Let's go, Gran'ma."

Billy helped Bess to her feet and they started towards the door. But before she left, she stopped…

"Just a moment."

…and walked back to the table. There was a mirror on the wall behind the table and a hairbrush on the table.

Bess picked up the brush and gave her hair a few strokes with the brush as she looked at herself in the mirror. Finally, satisfied with what she saw, she smiled at her image in the mirror. Then she put the hairbrush down and turned toward Billy.

"OK — now I'm ready."

Billy helped Bess out the front door of Doc Wilson's place.

The golden cloud was hovering right above them now.

As soon as Billy helped Bess mount "Peggy," two magnificent wings appeared and she miraculously started to look like the strong proud steed that we imagine Pegasus to be!

Bess looked down at Billy.

"Good-bye, Billy. I love you."

"Good-bye, Granma," Billy said with tears in his eyes. "I love you, too."

And then he spoke to the horse:

"You got an important passenger today, so take it real gentle, OK?"

Pegasus nodded and snorted, as if she had understood what he said.

Bess gently dug her heels into Pegasus and Pegasus majestically took off. But as she did, a large white feather fell out of one of her wings.

Billy reached down and picked up the feather with his right hand and then transferred it to his left hand.

Then he put his right hand up to shade his eyes as Pegasus and Bess flew upwards towards the golden cloud.

Just then, Doc Wilson pulled up in his car with Carol, Hector, Diane and Axton as passengers, but Billy was staring up into the sky so intently that he didn't even notice that they had arrived.

Up in the sky, Pegasus and Bess disappeared into the golden cloud.

Doc Wilson and the others all get out of the car.

Doc Wilson immediately went inside to check on Bess. Diane, Axton and Carol approached Billy.

Diane gave Billy a hug.

"Billy! I can't believe you won! Now I don't have to marry Mr. Bartlett, and we can keep the farm!"

But Billy was still staring up into the sky while holding the large feather in his left hand. Diane glanced up to see what Billy was looking at.

Doc Wilson reappeared and said solemnly, "I'm afraid that Bess has gone away."

Diane took a deep breath and said, "Oh, no."

Diane was immediately saddened to hear the news, but she was surprised to see that Billy was still smiling and staring up into the sky.

"Billy, dear, didn't you hear what Doc Wilson just said? Your Grandma Bess has gone away."

"I know," Billy said. "And there she is!"

He pointed up into the sky and all the others looked in the direction he is pointing, but all they could see was the golden cloud moving up towards heaven.

Billy had the large feather in his left hand and waved good-bye to Bess and Peggy with his right hand.

"Bye, Grandma! Bye, Peggy! Bye! Bye!"

~ ~

"And after that day," Grandpa said, "Billy never rode a horse again because he knew it would never be like the day he won the Labor Day steeplechase on the back of Pegasus."

Grandpa was still in his lounge chair with Alex seated on the floor next to the coffee table, finishing the last bite of a sandwich.

"Did that really happen, Grey-Granpa?"

"As sure as you're sittin' here today," his great-grandfather responded.

Just then, the doorbell rang.

Grandma came out of the kitchen and opened the front door to find Emily standing there.

"Just in time," said Grandma. "He just finished his story."

Emily came in and gave Grandma a hug.

"I hope he wasn't too much trouble."

"Not at all."

Emily went into the living room and said to Alex, "C'mon, dear — it's time to go home."

"OK," Alex replied.

Alex went over and gave his seated great-grandfather a hug.

"Thanks, Grey-Grandpa."

Alex looked Grandpa right in the eyes and they shared a moment of understanding.

"And thanks for the story," he continued.

"Anytime, anytime," his great-grandfather replied.

"C'mon — get your things," Emily sang out.

Alex picked up his canvas bag (which he had not even looked into).

Grandma went to the open front door to wave goodbye to them.

After they left, Emily said to Alex, "Now, that wasn't so bad, was it? Did you get to watch your tape?"

Emily looked in her purse for her car key. "Now where did I put that?

Just then, Alex said, "Hurry up, Mom! I don't wanna be late for my 'pointment!", with a combination of resolve and worry.

Grandma closed the door and walked into the living room where Grandpa was still seated.

"You never get tired of telling that story, do you?"

Grandpa leaned forward to prepare to stand up.

"Why not? It's the best story I know."

"But why do you always put in that stuff about Peggy flying?" Grandma asked.

Grandpa started to stand up...

"It don't hurt the story none."

...but he limped as he walked. His right leg was stiff — he couldn't straighten it completely.

"Besides, it makes the story more magical."

He walked over to a trophy on the mantle. It was the same trophy that, in the story, was given to Diane by Axton!

"C'mon, Billy," Grandma said. "I left a piece a pie for ya."

Grandma turned and headed into the kitchen.

"I'll be there in a minute, Carol," Grandpa Billy answered."

Grandpa Billy picked up the trophy and once again read the words printed on it:

"WINNER
WILLARD COUNTY
STEEPLECHASE
1935"

He put the trophy back down on the mantle.

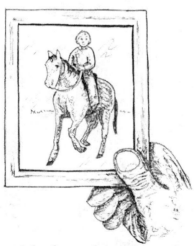

Then he picked up the picture frame that had fallen to the floor and looked at the photograph. It was the photograph that the photographer had taken at the end of the steeplechase race, and it showed the twelve-year-old Billy seated on Peggy!

Grandpa Billy looked to make sure that Grandma Carol was not around. Then he turned the picture frame around and removed the backing from the frame. Then, from inside the frame, he pulled out a big white feather!

He admired the feather a moment. Then he looked up (at heaven) and mouthed the words, "Thank you, Grandma."

Then Grandma Carol called out from the kitchen, "C'mon, Billy. It's getting cold!", bringing Grandpa Billy out of his reverie.

"Hold your horses! I'm coming!" he said.

He quickly put the feather back into the frame, put the backing of the frame back in place, and then returned the photo to the mantel.

Then he turned to go to the kitchen.

"Say, Carol — after dessert, what's say we put on some music and do a bit of dancin'?"

Hobbling, Grandpa Billy disappeared into the kitchen.

It's often easier to blame some thing or someone else for our misdeeds rather than taking responsibility for them. But, as Shakespeare wrote, "The fault is not in our stars but in ourselves."

Mr. Tushbottom's Collection

Mr. Nussbaum and Omar Haddid were neighbors. But despite the difference in their ages (Mr. Nussbaum was almost 70 years older than Omar), Omar visited his neighbor almost every day after school.

Mr. Nussbaum was so kind-hearted that he didn't even mind when some of the kids in the neighborhood called him "Mr. Tushbottom."

Mr. Nussbaum was a retired widower. (His wife had died at about the time Omar was born.) He and his wife had had one child, a daughter, but she had also died in a car accident when she was only 18, so Mr. Nussbaum was alone in the world.

Omar's father had died when he was only three years old, and his mother had not yet remarried. So now, at the age of six, Omar was the "man" of the family.

Omar also had an insatiable curiosity about the world, and Mr. Nussbaum seemed to be the only one in the neighborhood who could answer his questions (or who would take the time to do so).

And, if even Mr. Nussbaum didn't know the answer, he would help Omar by taking him to the library or a museum and together the two of them would always find the answer there. (Of course, Omar could hardly read at all. But although Mr. Nussbaum actually did almost all of the work, he had a way of making Omar feel like every accomplishment they shared was mostly Omar's to be proud of.)

Omar's mother worked full-time, but she trusted Mr. Nussbaum, so she was happy to have him look after Omar whenever he could.

Now, Mr. Nussbaum was also a collector — not because he liked to collect things but because he hated to throw things away!

For example, Mr. Nussbaum had once worked as a conductor on a train, and he had a menu from the dining car of every line he ever worked on. Not only that, but he also had a napkin to match each menu!

Mr. Nussbaum's home itself was sort of a cross between an antique shop and a museum of old souvenirs from his travels and other curiosities.

When Omar came to visit, all he had to do was point at something, say, "Tell me about that, Mr. Nussbaum," and before you could say "Albuquerque, Azusa and Cucamonga," Mr. Nussbaum would launch into a story of his travels to this state or that island, or how he had found a particular rock while climbing in the Alps or the Rockies or somewhere.

He may have looked old, Omar thought, but he could tell by the way Mr. Nussbaum talked that he had been young once too.

And, oh, how Mr. Nussbaum could talk! Usually, before Omar knew it, the afternoon had passed, and his mother was home, calling to tell him that his dinner was ready.

But one day when he showed up at Mr. Nussbaum's house, Omar did not seem as happy as usual. In fact, instead of greeting Mr. Nussbaum with a big smile, Omar didn't even look directly at him.

Mr. Nussbaum could immediately tell that his young friend had a problem that he needed to talk about, so he decided to do less talking today and more listening.

"Something botherin' you today, Omar?" he asked.

"Kinda," Omar replied.

"Well, why don't you tell me what 'kinda' happened?"

"Well, Mr. Tushbottom, I mean, Mr. Nussbaum, what happened was this," Omar began. "I was playing ball today at recess with my friend Minoru, and I threw the ball too hard at him, I guess, because it hit him in the eye and he had to go to the nurse's office."

"Did you mean to hurt him?" asked Mr. Nussbaum.

"No, and that's what's bothering me," Omar explained. "The other kids said that it was my fault he got hurt. But I said it wasn't my fault, it was Omar's fault, because he didn't catch the ball right.

"Anyway, it wasn't like I threw a rock at him, or something. I figure, if he got hurt, it must be because the ball was made too hard or he forgot to duck or something.

"I oughta sue the company that made the ball!"

Omar was quiet for a few moments, so Mr. Nussbaum asked him, "Did you feel bad when the other kids blamed you, Omar?"

"I did at the time, but I didn't like feeling that way, so I told them to get away from me, and they did."

They were both silent for a few seconds, and then Mr. Nussbaum said, "You know, Omar, not all 'bad feelings' are 'bad'. We were made to feel bad sometimes for a purpose."

"Whadya mean?" asked Omar, finally looking up at Mr. Nussbaum's face.

"Well, fr'instance, pain," explained Mr. Nussbaum. "We feel pain in order to know that we've been hurt and we need to do something to ameliora...uh, fix the pain, like put some medicine on it or something."

Omar picked his nose, trying to figure out what Mr. Nussbaum was getting at.

"And when we feel pain for hurting another person, that's a 'good' pain, because it's telling us that we hurt someone else, and we need to do something to help that person's hurt. The pain also helps to teach us not to do that kind of thing again."

Omar thought about this, but he still didn't see how it was his fault.

"Wait here a minute," said Mr. Nussbaum, and he got up and went into the other room.

After a couple minutes, he came back with a shoe box that was labeled "Things That Can Help You."

"Now look in this box," he began. "Do you see anything in this box that couldn't help you in some way if you were lost in the woods?"

Omar picked up the objects in the box, one by one, and examined them. The box contained just five objects: two rocks, a jackknife, a map, and a mirror.

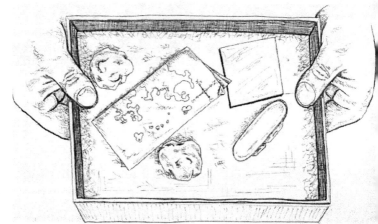

"Well, I understand how a map could help you if you were lost, Mr. Nussbaum. And a knife could help you cut up your food.

"But how could a mirror or a coupla rocks help you?"

"Well, think about it," Mr. Nussbaum explained. "These two rocks are the kind of rocks that, if you hit them together just right, can help you to start a fire to cook your food or keep you warm.

"And you can use a mirror to signal your position to rescuers."

Omar had to admit that, once again, Mr. Nussbaum was on target.

Then Mr. Nussbaum got up and left the room. This time he returned with another shoe box identical to the first one, but this one was labeled "Things That Can Hurt You."

And, as before, he asked Omar to examine the objects in the box but to tell him this time if there was anything in the box that couldn't hurt someone.

But when Omar looked in this box, he saw exactly the same five objects that he had just seen in the other shoe box!

"I don't get it, Mr. Nussbaum. This box has the same things as that box you just showed me."

"I know," he responded, "but try to answer the question anyway. Is there anything in the box that couldn't hurt someone?"

"Well," said Omar, brushing back his hair, "I understand how you could use a knife or a coupla rocks to hurt someone. But how could you hurt anyone with a map or a mirror?"

"Well," explained the old man, "if you broke the mirror, you could use it like a weapon to cut someone.

"And if you rolled the map up real tight," he demonstrated as he spoke, "you could use it like a stick to poke someone in the eye."

"Oh-oh," thought Omar. "He's got me again!"

"You see, Omar, there is no thing in the world that is either 'safe' or 'dangerous' by itself. Of course, we need to keep some things away from people who are irresponsible or can't make good decisions for themselves, like babies. But it is each individual's responsibility to decide how to use each thing, for good or for evil. And it's a good thing to feel shame if we hurt another person."

Omar sighed a sigh of recognition.

"Now what about a ball, Omar? Is a ball by itself something that can help you or hurt you?"

"No. Now I understand," replied Omar, looking down. "There's no good or bad in an object itself. Rather, it's how we decide to use a thing that determines if we acted in a good or bad way. So if we decide to use something to hurt someone, we have to take responsibility for our own actions."

"And in the same way," explained Mr. Nussbaum, "we all have lots of choices every day whether to use our lives for good or evil. And God gives us those choices because He wants us to learn to take responsibility for how we use the lives he gave us."

"I see what you mean, Mr. Nussbaum," conceded Omar. "You're right as usual."

"And we should be grateful to God for giving us those choices," Nussbaum continued. "Do you know why?"

Omar shook his head.

"I'll tell you why: Because every one of those choices is an opportunity for us to do something good."

They were both silent for a minute.

Finally, Omar spoke first.

"I'm really sorry that I hurt Minoru and that I said those bad things to my friends," Omar admitted. "I hope it's not too late to apologize to them."

"It never is," thought Mr. Nussbaum.

Just then the phone rang. It was Omar's Mom telling him that his dinner was ready.

So after thanking Mr. Nussbaum for being such a good friend, Omar left for home.

Mr. Nussbaum put away the shoe box with the two tops, one labeled "Things That Can Help You" and the other labeled "Things That Can Hurt You."

But before he began to fix his own dinner, he went into the den, sat down in front of the pictures of his late wife and daughter, and told them about the good thing he had been able to do that day.

We all like to dream how our lives could be better than they are, but there's only one sure-fire way to make our lives better...

The Bottle with the Strings Attached

One morning, when he was supposed to be in school, Ramesh was instead sleeping on the beach. He often came down to the beach on school days to practice his "I Wishes" (you know, "I wish I was smarter", "I wish I was older", and so on) because there was hardly anyone else there.

Well, this day, when Ramesh woke up from his nap, he happened to look out into the surf, and he saw what he was sure was a bottle. Thinking it might contain a message from a faraway place, he waded out into the surf and brought it back to the shore.

When he opened the bottle he didn't find a message, but what happened next surprised Ramesh so much that he jumped backwards, farther than he had ever jumped forwards in his life!

A genie popped out of the bottle! (Ramesh knew right away that he was a genie because it said "Genie U." right on the front of his cap, and "Your wish is my command" on the front of his sweatshirt. Even though Ramesh often skipped school, he wasn't that dumb.)

"Hi!" said the genie. "Am I ever glad I found you! I've been drifting around in that bottle ever since that Aladdin kid tossed me off his flying carpet. To tell you the truth," he whispered conspiratorially, "I was beginning to get seasick."

(Now if Ramesh had been really smart, he might have asked himself right then and there why anyone would have thrown away a bottle with a genie inside it, but, he wasn't and he didn't, so we still have a story to tell.)

"Wow! Are you a real genie?" he asked. "Like they have in the TV commercials?"

"What is 'TV'?" asked the genie.

"Never mind," said Ramesh. "Listen, are you the kind of genie that can grant me a wish?"

"Is there any other kind?" said the genie proudly.

"Wow wow wow, oh my gosh, oh my gosh, oh man oh man oh man," screamed Ramesh as he danced around in the sand. "I can't believe it, I can't believe it, I can't believe it!"

"Much more demonstrative than that Aladdin kid," thought the genie.

"All my life, I've been hoping that something like this would happen to me," screamed Ramesh. Finally, finished with his dance of joy, he turned back to the genie. "So can I have three wishes?"

"Well, we used to grant three wishes," the genie explained, "but with inflation and all, I'm afraid that now we can only afford to grant one."

"Well, that's better than nothing," thought Ramesh.

Now he had to think very carefully — what should his one and only wish be?

Of course, Ramesh first tried to wish for more wishes.

The genie shook his head and smiled. (He had been through this before.) Then he said that, unfortunately, due to union rules, he couldn't allow that.

So Ramesh then declared: "I wish to be the richest person in the world!"

"Of course, I could grant you that wish," said the genie, who obviously wasn't as dumb as he looked. "But before I do, I am required to warn you of some of the bad things that, from my experience, always seem to go along with that wish."

"Like what?"

"Well, for one thing you will never have any real friends again, because only bad people who just want something from you will try to be your friends. Good people will be afraid to bother you or will be afraid that you wouldn't be interested in getting to know them. So, soon you won't trust anyone, and you won't have any friends at all."

"Hmm," thought Ramesh. "That wouldn't be any good."

Then, after thinking for a minute, he said, "OK, then I'd like to be the most powerful person in the world!"

"Of course, I could grant you that wish," said the genie, once again. "But before I do, I am required to warn you of some of the bad things that, from my experience, always seem to go along with that wish."

"Like what?"

"Well, if you become the most powerful person in the world, after a short time you are sure to become bored because you will be able to get everything you want so easily. And then you are sure to abuse your power, and people will begin to hate you and start plotting to kill you."

"Well, then, I wish to become immortal and live forever!"

The genie started his spiel again, "Of course, I could grant you that wish...."

"OK, OK, just cut to the chase," interjected Ramesh, now getting quite annoyed.

"Well, if you were to live forever, you would no longer value life, and, eventually, you would get bored again. In addition, you would eventually see everyone you loved or cared about get old and die, so you would stop trying to get close to other people. Likewise, other people would become envious and would stay away from you, so you would eventually become an immortal but bitter hermit."

"OK, then, I'd like to have the most beautiful woman in the world fall madly in love with me. What could be wrong with that?" demanded Ramesh.

"Well, the problem with that," explained the patient genie, "is that she will continue to love you even after she loses her beauty and you are no longer interested in her, for, after all, most beautiful women are not very interesting after they lose their beauty. And she will follow you and cling to you for the rest of your life. Eventually she'd start to stalk you and you would have to get a restraining order against her, which, as you know, rarely does any good."

Now Ramesh was starting to get frustrated because he could see where this conversation was going.

"OK, how about an expensive brand-new car?"

"Not only high insurance rates and maintenance costs, but people will constantly be trying to steal it, and one day someone might try to carjack it while you were in it," replied the genie smugly.

"High intelligence?"

"If I gave you high intelligence, not only would other people start to have high expectations of you that you could never live up to, but you'd become bored with other people and cynical about life."

"Could you make me older?"

"I could, but then think of all of the pleasure you would miss."

"Then could you make me younger?"

"Yes, of course, but then think of all the pain you would have to go through all over again."

This back-and-forth conversation went on for most of the afternoon, with Ramesh finally conceding that there were negative things associated with every thing he asked for.

So, finally, Ramesh asked the genie, "Well, is there anything, in your experience, that anyone has ever wished for that actually worked out well for him?"

The genie thought a minute, and then said, "Yes, I remember one girl who had the wisdom to ask, not that her wishes be immediately granted, but that she would gain the self-confidence and strength to work tirelessly to achieve her dreams."

So, Ramesh took the genie's advice and wished for those things.

Then, just like Aladdin had done, Ramesh thanked the genie and put him back in the bottle. Next he threw the bottle back into the sea, and he watched as it drifted away until it was out of sight.

Finally, exhausted, he lay down to rest again.

After just a few minutes, he woke up and, figuring that by now it must be time for dinner, he rushed home.

But when he got home, he was surprised to find his mother just preparing lunch.

"What are you doing home from school so early?" she asked.

Thinking quickly, he said, "Oh, I forgot something I need."

So he grabbed a paper from his room and ran off to school.

And, from that day on, he never skipped school again, and he even became one of the better students.

And although he never stopped dreaming, Ramesh found that working toward achieving his dreams gave him the greatest pleasure of all, just like the genie said it would!

We all feel bad when we hear that someone has been the victim of a crime, but aren't we all in some way victims of every crime?

The Billion-Dollar Bullet

James Johnson only had one bullet in his gun, so he wanted to make sure he used it well.

It was a warm summer evening, and James was walking down the main street of Wrightville, Indiana. The pleasant Mid-Western city of nearly 30,000 inhabitants was the kind of small town that America was built on and that all too rarely exists anymore. It was large enough to allow employment opportunities for the young people yet small enough so that it seemed like everyone knew everyone else.

The main street of Wrightville was a popular place to shop, to go on a date, or just to stroll on warm summer evenings. Not only did the stores stay open late in the summer, but there was also the Wrightville Cinema (two screens), the Wrightville Creamery ("GREAT Cherry-Cola Floats!"), the Wrightville Bowling Alley, and Aunt Mary's Home-Cooking Family Style Restaurant ("Try Our Pie!").

In fact, Main Street was the kind of place where you could drop off your teenage son or daughter after dinner and not worry about what would happen to them before you picked them up there later that night. People came to Main Street to see and be seen.

But James had other things on his mind. He had just spotted someone from a rival gang across the street.

James had been angry all day. A member of the rival gang had "dissed" one of James's friends at summer school that day, so James felt he had to get revenge.

And he knew just what he would do: He would take out his gun, aim carefully, and "POW!", blow that sucker away.

Unfortunately, his aim was poor and he would miss the rival gang member. But before the crowds of people on the street would even realize what was happening, the rival gang member would take out his own gun and return the fire: "Pow! Pow! Pow! Pow!"

His aim was also bad, however, and instead of hitting James, he would hit two innocent bystanders: John, a forty-year-old married man, and Mary Alice, a sixteen-year-old high school cheer leader.

By the time the police arrived, James had fled, but he was soon arrested. He was eventually tried at a cost of close to $50,000, and sentenced to 21 years in prison (but was released after serving only eight years) at a cost to taxpayers of over $150,000.

This was too bad, because he had hoped to use his athletic talents to get a scholarship to the state university, get a bachelor's degree, become a pro-football player and then go to law school. (Total lifetime earnings lost: almost twenty million dollars.)

But now all those dreams had gone "up in smoke."

Sadly, because of his arrest, James would not have any children, either. And this was especially unfortunate because, if he had not been arrested, he would have married and had three children. One son would have become a teacher and writer, a daughter would have become a doctor, and the other son would have become the first African-American mayor of Wrightville.

In addition, if James had had children, one of his grandsons, Marshall (the son of the Mayor), would have become first a U.S. Senator, then the first African-American Vice-President of the United States, and, eventually, President when the elected President died in office. And, as President, he would have helped find a peaceful solution to the African Crisis of 2077.

John, the man who was hit, did not survive, and he left behind a widow and two children. Unfortunately, he had not taken out any life insurance, so his widow had to move out of their house and go on welfare.

And, because of John's death, instead of graduating from college as they would have done, both of his children got pregnant and dropped out of high school.

Luckily the teenage girl, Mary Alice, survived, but she was seriously injured. In fact, her hospital bills totaled over $200,000 and her life-long rehabilitation costs were over $1,000,000. (This, of course, did not include her life-time loss of wages.) And since she had no health insurance, the county government had to pay the entire costs, which meant it had less money to invest in preventive health programs such as immunization of poor children.

Also, because of her injuries, Mary Alice could not have any children, and she would never marry. So she would never bear her son Conrad, who would have been the best basketball player to come out of Indiana since Larry Bird.

Mary Alice would also never achieve her life-long dream of becoming a nurse.

Because of her injuries, none of that would happen now.

The rival gang member, Ernesto, was already long gone by the time police arrived. (He was afraid that he might have been recognized by someone in the crowd, so he figured he'd better skip town.)

Of course, Ernesto was eventually caught after committing a series of bank robberies (including three in which innocent people were injured) while on the run (cost to banks and in medical costs: almost $500,000).

Ernesto was brought back to Wrightville for trial. (Total cost to all law enforcement agencies for his capture and arrest: $22,000.)

The first trial ended in a hung jury, but Ernesto was convicted in the second trial. That conviction was overturned on a technicality, but his conviction in the third trial was upheld. (Total cost for guards, judges, court reporters, prosecuting attorneys, court-appointed defense attorneys, court room costs, transcripts, and so on, for the three trials: over $1,000,000.)

Ernesto was sentenced to death for his crimes, but the appeals process dragged on for years. (Total cost to taxpayers of his incarceration and appeals: over $2,500,000.)

Meanwhile, the shooting had a profound effect on not only downtown Wrightville, but on the entire community as well: when people heard about the shooting, they stopped coming to visit the downtown area at night.

In an attempt to try and reassure the public, several of the store owners hired armed guards (at $12.50 an hour) to stand outside the doors of their shops, but it did no good. In fact, it had the opposite effect. Several of the stores, which counted on the profits from staying open late on the long summer evenings, ended up going out of business and were boarded up.

Many of the shops that used to line Main Street had employed local teenagers in the summer months, so when the shops closed, teenage unemployment rose, leading even more of the young people to join gangs. In addition, many of the shops had bought their goods from small family-run factories in the surrounding area, which also therefore suffered from the decrease in business.

Then, all of a sudden, graffiti started to show up on the boarded-up store fronts, declaring the street to be the turf of one gang or another. Shoplifting also increased, which forced the shop owners to raise their prices, not only to make up for the cost of the stolen goods but also to pay for expensive new electronic security systems. The higher prices, in turn, cut down on business even more.

So, before anyone realized what had happened, the street had deteriorated to the point where most of the businesses remaining were either bars, porn shops, or cheap hotels that rented rooms by the hour.

Of course, this put a lot of people out of work and also affected the property values of the homes surrounding the downtown area. This, in turn, lowered the amount of property taxes that the city could collect, which led to a cutback in city services such as trash collection and police on duty. Even the hours the libraries were open were cut back.

With lower property values and fewer public services, the entire city started to deteriorate. Young people who wanted a secure future began to move out of Wrightville to the big cities to look for work. And because it was losing its most talented young people, Wrightville deteriorated even more.

After a while, the only people who were left in Wrightville were the people who were too old or too poor to move away.

So, in the end, the total cost (including the cost of the African War of 2078) of that one bullet fired out of James's gun would come to over a billion dollars. And this does not include the damage done to the lives of all those who knew either the culprits or the victims, nor the damage done to the ability of the townspeople to enjoy the town where they lived.

But luckily, James thought better of it, and decided not to pull out his gun and fire, so none of those terrible things happened.

The End

Richard Showstack is a full-time writer in Southern California. If you would like to get in touch with him, please send your e-mail to: Fables4Teenagers@AOL.com

Books from Science & Humanities Press

HOW TO TRAVEL—A Guidebook for Persons with a Disability – Fred Rosen (1997) ISBN 1-888725-05-2, 5½ X 8¼, 120 pp, $9.95 18-point large print edition (1998) ISBN 1-888725-17-6 7X8, 120 pp, $19.95

HOW TO TRAVEL in Canada—A Guidebook for A Visitor with a Disability – Fred Rosen (2000) ISBN 1-888725-26-5, 5½X8¼, 180 pp, $14.95 MacroPrintBooks™ edition (2001) ISBN 1-888725-30-3 7X8, 16 pt, 200 pp, $19.95

AVOIDING Attendants from HELL: A Practical Guide to Finding, Hiring & Keeping Personal Care Attendants 2nd Edn—June Price, (2002), accessible plastic spiral bind, ISBN 1-888725-72-9 8¼X10½, 125 pp, $16.95, School/library edition (2002) ISBN 1-888725-60-5, 8¼X6½, 200 pp, $18.95

The Bridge Never Crossed—A Survivor's Search for Meaning. Captain George A. Burk (1999) The inspiring story of George Burk, lone survivor of a military plane crash, who overcame extensive burn injuries to earn a presidential award and become a highly successful motivational speaker. ISBN 1-888725-16-8, 5½X8¼, 170 pp, illustrated. $16.95 MacroPrintBooks™ Edition (1999) ISBN 1-888725-28-1 $24.95

Value Centered Leadership—A Survivor's Strategy for Personal and Professional Growth—Captain George A. Burk (2003) Principles of Leadership & Total Quality Management applied to all aspects of living. ISBN 1-888725-59-1, 5½X8¼, 120 pp, $16.95

Paul the Peddler or The Fortunes of a Young Street Merchant—Horatio Alger, jr A Classic reprinted in accessible large type, (1998 MacroPrintBooks™ reprint in 24-point type) ISBN 1-888725-02-8, 8¼X10½, 276 pp, $16.95

The Wisdom of Father Brown—G.K. Chesterton (2000) A Classic collection of detective stories reprinted in accessible 22-point type ISBN 1-888725-27-3 8¼X10½, 276 pp, $18.95

24-point Gospel—The Big News for Today – The Gospel according to Matthew, Mark, Luke & John (KJV) in 24-point typeType is about 1/3 inch high. Now, people with visual disabilities like macular degeneration can still use this important reference. "Giant print" books are usually 18 pt. or less ISBN 1-888725-11-7, 8¼X10½, 512 pp, $24.95

Buttered Side Down - Short Stories by Edna Ferber (BeachHouse Booksreprint 2000) A classic collection of stories by the beloved author of Showboat, Giant, and Cimarron. ISBN 1-888725-43-5, 5½X8¼, 190 pp, $12.95 MacroPrintBooks™ Edition (2000) ISBN 1-888725-40-0 7X8¼,16 pt, 240 pp $18.95

The Four Million: The Gift of the Magi & other favorites. Life in New York City around 1900—O. Henry. MacroPrintBooks™ reprint (2001) ISBN 1-888725-41-9 7X8¼, 16 pt, 270 pp $18.95; ISBN 1-888725-03-6, 8¼X10½, 22 pt, 300pp, $22.95

Bar-20: Hopalong Cassidy's Rustler Roundup—Clarence Mulford (reprint 2000). Classical Western Tale. Not the TV version. ISBN 1-888725-34-6

5½X8¼, 223 pp, $12.95 MacroPrintBooks™ edition
ISBN 1-888725-42-7, 8¼X6½, 16 pt, 385pp, $18.95

Nursing Home – Ira Eaton, PhD, (1997) You will
be moved and disturbed by this novel. ISBN 1-
888725-01-X, 5½X8¼, 300 pp, $12.95
MacroPrintBooks™ edition (1999) ISBN 1-888725-
23-0,8¼X10½, 16 pt, 330 pp, $18.95

Perfect Love-A Novel by Mary Harvatich (2000)
Love born in an orphanage endures ISBN 1-888725-
29-X 5½X8¼, 200 pp, $12.95 MacroPrintBooks™
edition (2000) ISBN 1-888725-15-X, 8¼X10½, 16 pt,
200 pp, $18.95

The Essential Simply Speaking Gold – Susan
Fulton, (1998) How to use IBM's popular speech
recognition package for dictation rather than
keyboarding. Dozens of screen shots and
illustrations. ISBN 1-888725-08-7 8¼ X8, 124 pp,
$18.95

Begin Dictation Using ViaVoice Gold -2nd
Edition– Susan Fulton, (1999), Covers ViaVoice 98
and other versions of IBM's popular continuous
speech recognition package for dictation rather
than keyboarding. Over a hundred screen shots
and illustrations. ISBN 1-888725-22-2, 8¼X8, 260
pp, $28.95

Ropes and Saddles—Andy Polson (2001) Cowboy
(and other) poems by Andy Polson. Reminiscences
of the Wyoming poet. ISBN 1-888725-39-7, 5½ X
8¼, 100 pp, $9.95

Tales from the Woods of Wisdom - (book I) - Richard Tichenor (2000) In a spirit someplace between The Wizard of Oz and The Celestine Prophecy, this is more than a childrens' fable of life in the deep woods. ISBN 1-888725-37-0, 5½X8¼, 185 pp, $16.95 MacroPrintBooks™ edition (2001) ISBN 1-888725-50-8 6X8¼, 16 pt, 270 pp $24.95

Me and My Shadows—Shadow Puppet Fun for Kids of All Ages - Elizabeth Adams, Revised Edition by Dr. Bud Banis (2000) A thoroughly illustrated guide to the art of shadow puppet entertainment using tools that are always at hand wherever you go. A perfect gift for children and adults. ISBN 1-888725-44-3, 7X8¼, 67 pp, 12.95 MacroPrintBooks™ edition (2002) ISBN 1-888725-78-8 8½X11 lay-flat spiral, 18 pt, 67 pp, $16.95

MamaSquad! (2001) Hilarious novel by Clarence Wall about what happens when a group of women from a retirement home get tangled up in Army Special Forces. ISBN 1-888725-13-3 5½ X8¼, 200 pp, $14.95 MacroPrintBooks™ edition (2001) ISBN 1-888725-14-1 8¼X6½ 16 pt, 300 pp, $24.95

Virginia Mayo—The Best Years of My Life (2002) Autobiography of film star Virginia Mayo as told to LC Van Savage. From her early days in Vaudeville and the Muny in St Louis to the dozens of hit motion pictures, with dozens of photographs. ISBN 1-888725-53-2, 5½ X 8¼, 200 pp, $16.95

The Job—Eric Whitfield (2001) A story of self-discovery in the context of the death of a grandfather.. A book to read and share in times of change and Grieving. ISBN 1-888725-68-0, 5½ X 8¼, 100 pp, $12.95 MacroPrintBooks™ edition (2001) ISBN 1-888725-69-9, 8¼X6½, 18 pt, 150 pp, $18.95

Plague Legends: from the Miasmas of Hippocrates to the Microbes of Pasteur-Socrates Litsios D.Sc. (2001) Medical progress from early history through the 19th Century in understanding origins and spread of contagious disease. A thorough but readable and enlightening history of medicine. Illustrated, Bibliography, Index ISBN 1-888725-33-8, 6¼X8¼, 250pp, $24.95

Sexually Transmitted Diseases—Symptoms, Diagnosis, Treatment, Prevention-2nd Edition – NIAID Staff, Assembled and Edited by R.J.Banis, PhD, (2005) Teacher friendly —free to copy for education. Illustrated with more than 50 photographs of lesions, ISBN 1-888725-58-3, 8¼X6½, 200 pp, $18.95

The Stress Myth -Serge Doublet, PhD (2000) A thorough examination of the concept that 'stress' is the source of unexplained afflictions. Debunking mysticism, psychologist Serge Doublet reviews the history of other concepts such as 'demons', 'humors', 'hysteria' and 'neurasthenia' that had been placed in this role in the past, and provides an alternative approach for more success in coping with life's challenges. ISBN 1-888725-36-2, 5½X8¼, 280 pp, $24.95

Behind the Desk Workout – Joan Guccione, OTR/C, CHT (1997) ISBN 1-888725-00-1, Reduce risk of injury by exercising regularly at your desk. Over 200 photos and illustrations. (lay-flat spiral) 8¼X10½, 120 pp, $34.95 Paperback edition, (2000) ISBN 1-888725-25-7 $24.95

Republican or Democrat? (2004) Moses Sanchez, who describes himself as "a Black Hispanic" thinks for himself, questions the stereotypes, examines the facts and makes his own decision. Early Editions Books ISBN 1-888725-32-X 5½X8¼, 176pp pp, $14.95

Journey to a Closed City with the International Executive Service Corps—Russell R. Miller (2004) ISBN 1-888725-94-X, Describes the adventures of a retired executive volunteering with the senior citizens' equivalent of the Peace Corp as he applies his professional skills in a former Iron Curtain city emerging into the dawn of a new economy.This book is essential reading for anyone approaching retirement who is interested in opportunities to exercise skills to "do good" during expense-paid travel to intriguing locations. Journey to A Closed City should also appeal to armchair travelers eager to explore far-off corners of the world in our rapidly-evolving global community. paperback, 5½X8¼,270pp,$16.95 **MacroPrintBooks**™ edition (2004) ISBN 1-888725-94-8, 8¼X6½, 18 pt, 150 pp, $24.95

Inaugural Addresses: Presidents of the United States from George Washington to 2008 -3rd Edition– Robert J. Banis, PhD, CMA, Ed. (2005) Extensively illustrated, includes election statistics, Vice- presidents, principal opponents, Index. coupons for update supplements for the next two elections. ISBN 1-59630-004-3, 6¼X8¼, 350pp, $18.95

Copyright Issues for Librarians, Teachers & Authors–R.J. Banis, PhD, (Ed). 2nd Edn (2001) Protecting your rights, respecting others'. Information condensed from the Library of Congress, copyright registration forms. ISBN 1-888725-62-1, 5¼X8¼, 60 pp, booklet. $4.95

50 Things You Didn't Learn in School–But Should Have: Little known facts that still affect our world today (2005) by John Naese, . ISBN 1-888725-49-4, 5½X8¼, 200 pp, illustrated. $16.95

Eudora Light™ v 3.0 Manual (Qualcomm 1996) ISBN 1-888725-20-6½, extensively illustrated. 135 pp, 5½ X 8¼, $9.95

Rhythm of the Sea —Shari Cohen (2001). Delightful collection of heartwarming stories of life relationships set in the context of oceans and lakes. Shari Cohen is a popular author of Womens' magazine articles and contributor to the Chicken Soup for the Soul series. ISBN 1-888725-55-9, 8X6.5 150 pp, $14.95 MacroPrintBooks™ edition (2001) ISBN 1-888725-63-X, 8¼X6½, 16 pt, 250 pp, $24.95

To Norma Jeane With Love, Jimmie -Jim Dougherty as told to LC Van Savage (2001) ISBN 1-888725-51-6 The sensitive and touching story of Jim Dougherty's teenage bride who later became Marilyn Monroe. Dozens of photographs. "The Marilyn Monroe book of the year!" As seen on TV. 5½X8¼, 200 pp, $16.95 MacroPrintBooks™ edition ISBN 1-888725-52-4, 8¼X6½, 16 pt, 290pp, $24.95

Riverdale Chronicles—Charles F. Rechlin (2003). Life, living and character studies in the setting of the Riverdale Golf Club by Charles F. Rechlin 5½ X 8¼, 100 pp ISBN: 1-888725-84-2 $14.95

MacroPrintBooks™ edition (2003) 16 pt. 8¼X6½, 16 pt, 350 pp ISBN: 1-888725-85-0 $24.95

Bloodville — Don Bullis (2002) Fictional adaptation of the Budville, NM murders by New Mexico crime historian, Don Bullis. 5½ X 8¼, 350 pp ISBN: 1-888725-75-3 $14.95

MacroPrintBooks™ edition (2003) 16 pt. 8¼X11 460pp ISBN: 1-888725-76-1 $24.95

The Cut—John Evans (2003). Football, Mystery and Mayhem in a highschool setting by John Evans ISBN: 1-888725-82-6 5½ X 8¼, 100 pp $14.95

MacroPrintBooks™ edition (2003) 16 pt. ISBN: 1-888725-83-4 $24.95

The Way It Was-- Nostalgic Tales of Hotrods and Romance Chuck Klein (2003) Series of hotrod stories by author of Circa 1957 in collaboration with noted illustrator Bill Lutz BeachHouse Books edition 5½ X 8¼, 200 pp ISBN: 1-888725-86-9 $14.95

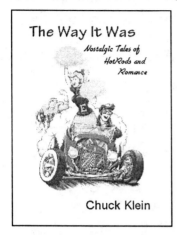

MacroPrintBooks™ edition (2003) 16 pt. 8¼X6½, 350pp ISBN: 1-888725-87-7 $24.95

"...a delightful mix of anecdote, observation, and social history. A book so masterfully written, you can almost smell new upholstery on the street rod. This is definitely the best read..."

Paul Taylor, Publisher. Route 66 Magazine

"...a classic recipe for hours of delightful entertainment.... If this is your first time reading Chuck Klein, it¹s just like eating chocolate. Once you have the first bite, you know you¹ll be coming back for more. "

Carl Cartisano, Cruisin¹ Style Magazine

Route 66 books by Michael Lund

Growing Up on Route 66 —Michael Lund (2000) ISBN 1-888725-31-1 Novel evoking fond memories of what it was like to grow up alongside "America's Highway" in 20th Century Missouri. (Trade paperback) 5½ X8¼, 260 pp, $14.95

MacroPrintBooks™ edition (2001) ISBN 1-888725-45-1 8¼X6½, 16 pt, 330 pp, $24.95

Route 66 Kids —Michael Lund (2002) ISBN 1-888725-70-2 Sequel to *Growing Up on Route 66*, continuing memories of what it was like to grow up alongside "America's Highway" in 20th Century Missouri. (Trade paperback) 5½ X8¼, 270 pp, $14.95 **MacroPrintBooks**™ edition (2002) ISBN 1-888725-71-0 8¼X6½, 16 pt, 350 pp, $24.95

A Left-hander on Route 66--Michael Lund (2003) ISBN 1-888725-88-5. Twenty years after the fact, left-hander Hugh Noone appeals a wrongful conviction that detoured him from "America's Main Street" and put him in jail. But revealing the details of the past and effecting a resolution of his case mean a dramatic rearrangement of his world, including troubled relationships with three women: Linda Roy, Patty Simpson, and Karen Murphy. (Trade paperback) 5½ X8¼, 270 pp, $14.95 **MacroPrintBooks**™ edition (2002) ISBN 1-888725-89-3 8¼X6½, 16 pt, 350 pp, $24.95

Miss Route 66--Michael Lund (2004) ISBN: 1-888725-96-6. In this novel, Susan Bell tells the story of her candidacy in Fairfield, Missouri's annual beauty contest. Now married and with teenage children in St. Louis, she recounts her youthful adventure in this small town along "America's Highway." At the same time, she plans a return to Fairfield in order to right injustices she feels were done to some young contestants in the Miss Route 66 Pageant. Throughout this journey she wonders what, if anything, was feminine in the "Mother Road" of the 1950s. (Trade paperback) 5½ X8¼, 270 pp, $14.95. **MacroPrintBooks**™ edition (2002) ISBN 1-888725-97-4 8¼X6½, 16 pt, 350 pp, $24.95.

AudioBook on CD-- Miss Route 66 ISBN: 1-888725-12-5 by Michael Lund unabridged 5 CD's -- 7 Hours running time. $24.95

Route 66 Spring-- Michael Lund (2004) ISBN: 1-888725-98-2. The lives of four young Missourians are changed when a bottle comes to the surface of one of the state's many natural springs. Inside is a letter written by a girl a dozen years after the end of the Civil War. Lucy Rivers Johns ' epistle contains a sad story of family failure and a powerful plea for help. This message from the last century crystallizes the individual frustrations of Janet Masters, Freddy Sills, Louis Clark, and Roberta Green, another group of Route 66 kids. Their response to the past charts a bold path into the future, a path inspired by the Mother Road itself. (Trade paperback) 5½ X8¼, 270 pp, $14.95. **MacroPrintBooks**™ edition (2002) ISBN 1-888725-99-0. 8¼X6½, 16 pt, 350 pp, $24.95.

Route 66 to Vietnam Michael Lund (2004) ISBN 1-59630-000-0 This novel takes characters from earlier works in the Route 66 Novel Series farther west than Los Angeles, official destination of the famous highway, Route 66. Mark Landon and Billy Rhodes find the values they grew up on challenged by America's role in Southeast Asia. But elements of their upbringing represented by the Mother Road also sustain them in ways they could never have anticipated. . (Trade paperback) 5½ X8¼, 270 pp, $14.95. **MacroPrintBooks**™ edition (2004) ISBN 1-59630-001-9. 8¼X6½, 16 pt, 350 pp, $24.95.

Our books are guaranteed:

If a book has a defect, or doesn't hold up under normal use, or if you are unhappy in any way with one of our books, we are interested to know about it and will replace it and credit reasonable return shipping costs. Products with publisher defects (i.e., books with missing pages, etc.) may be returned at any time without authorization. However, we request that you describe the problem, to help us to continuously improve.

Books by Richard Showstack

The Gift of the Magic -and other enchanting character-building stories for smart teenage girls who want to grow up to be strong women. Richard Showstack, (2004) 1-888725-64-8 5½ X8¼, 145 pp, $14.95 **MacroPrintBooks**[TM] edition ISBN 1-888725-65-8¼X6½, 16 pt, 280 pp, $24.95

A Horse Named Peggy-and other enchanting character-building stories for smart teenage boys who want to grow up to be good men. Richard Showstack, (2004) 1-888725-66-4. 5½ X8¼, 145 pp, $14.95 **MacroPrintBooks**[TM] edition ISBN 1-888725-67, 8¼X6½, 16 pt, 280 pp, $24.95

Order Form

Item	Each	Quantity	Amount
Missouri (only) sales tax 6.075%			
Priority Shipping			$4.00
	Total		
Name Address			

BeachHouse Books   PO Box 7151
 Chesterfield,MO 63006-7151
 (636) 394-4950